Jon de Graaff

MIRACLES FROM PETROGRAD
TO THE OUTBACK

Friends of the Tsar

To find out more about this book or
to contact the author, please visit:
www.vividpublishing.com.au/friendsofthetsar

Copyright © 2021 Jon de Graaff

ISBN: 978-1-922409-05-8
Published by Vivid Publishing
A division of Fontaine Publishing Group
P.O. Box 948, Fremantle
Western Australia 6959
www.vividpublishing.com.au

 A catalogue record for this
book is available from the
National Library of Australia

Introduction

A young baroness falls in love with an Australian when he visits a prominent Russian baron at his country estate. The situation in Russia, consequential to the Tsar's heavy-handed rule and war, was progressively getting worse. Two prominent aristocratic Russian families take measures to stay at their friend's station in Australia and return when things look like settling down, but they find themselves in the middle of a revolution that will test their faith.

The author tells of the many miracles he had been blessed with in his personal life, most of which are so profound in that they are logic-defying. The miracles suggest that, had they not been divinely ordered, the author and his family would not be here today.

A host of funny and dramatic real-life situations are narrated through the Australian character, Blue. The author believes that they have been shown to him by the divine to share with the world in a way that will give one food for thought about the many dangerous situations that will no doubt be encountered sometime in one's life.

Baron George Alexander Zuckschwerdt's ancestor was the personal bodyguard of Alexander the Great. George married the author's grandmother, Vera, at the age of eighteen.

Just hours before the Petrograd Soviet became an official power, the two families fled onboard their friends ship and endured dangerous situations, one of which turned into a deadly game of bluff between the ship's captain and the skipper of a German U-boat. The confrontation would test the nerve and skills of the ship's captain, a retired Russian commander, and of his noble friends. All the men, having military experience, would rally to try to prevent a potential routine deck gun attack on the ship to sink her.

The objective of this book is to try to help people gain some spiritual awareness, bring attention to the ever-present dangers in nature, and to inspire those who have their own challenges in life. People whose lives have been dealt a blow and have fought back are encouraged to be seen, so that they, too, can inspire others.

It is important for people to tell their family's remarkable stories before they take them to the grave with them.

The aristocratic Zuckschwerdt family at their country estate near Petrograd, Russia, in 1917. They were friends of the Tsar. Below, Vera Orloff, left, then seventeen, and sister Monica Sophie, sixteen. Vera married Baron George Zuckschwerdt, grandparents of the author.

One

Lovesick Vera in wolf attack, Russia, 1916

In the thick snow that fell on the country estate belonging to young George's father, Baron Alexander Zuckschwerdt, near Petrograd (St. Petersburg) in Russia on a bleak afternoon in early January 1916, lay a pack of desperately hungry wolves. They were not interested in George's fiancée, seventeen-year-old Vera Orloff, who was staying at the estate with her father, Nikolai, it was the young goat kids inside the barn she was on her way to feed that they wanted.

"Have you seen Vera, Mum?" asked George when he walked into the huge kitchen after putting on his work coat to groom his father's Australian Waler horses. He was worried that she was not as alert as she let on, for he knew that she was lovesick over him, and she was so used to life in her family's mansion in Petrograd and had no wild animals around to contend with.

"She went to feed the animals. I would've stopped her if I knew you were outside," said Adelaide who was usually more prudent and would normally have investigated everything thoroughly to protect the wellbeing of the family, but the potential for injudiciousness was at an all-time high due to the unrest.

"Heck! How many times have I told her?" he complained as he ran outside and headed for the barn, one hundred yards away. "Vera! Vera!" he shouted. Being a loving, caring, devoted, and protective aristocrat, his instincts vibrated to a higher frequency. His innate spiritual gladiator took the reins and dragged him along to where he had to go and told him to do what he had to do. Since he had been with Vera, he has been in tune with his higher self.

He heard the commotion of the horses reducing the stables to splinters and the loud barking of the husky team that warned of big trouble coming from inside the barn. He unholstered his revolver and made haste. He was not going to fail his beloved Vera. She taught him that there were more important things in life than studying and making money, a vicious cycle in which he was trapped, but now he embraced his awakening at a soul level and could now see the positive rewards.

She was going to open one of the two outward-swinging barn doors to see what was spooking the horses. She thought, "Oh, no! I didn't bring my gun! What's in there?" She looked around at the snow-covered trees that were a short distance from the side of the barn toward the end of the house. "I'd better run back to the house," she though as reality crept back into the corridors of her love fantasy temple.

"Vera! Vera!"

"George! Something's spooking the horses and dogs!"

He was a short distance away when he saw a wolf emerge from the tree line and make a run for her. "Look out!" He stopped, initiated a shooting stance, and shot one round off at the beast as it leapt to attack her. He knew not what he was doing, as the gladiator was in full control. His actions were that of a fearless, strong, grounded, and focussed warrior who would sacrifice his life to protect his loved ones.

She saw the beast drop at her feet when she turned to see what he was shooting at. Through shock, she threw her back against one of the doors. "My God!" she cried as her hands went to her mouth when she saw it. She looked up to see if there were any more around before she looked back at him.

"Oh, Vera! He was going to have you for lunch!" He went to her. "Why are the Walers still demolishing the stables? Is there something in there?" he thought, keeping an eye out for any sign of danger. The stables were inside the huge barn.

"I know, I was warned about this," she said to him

and shook her head.

"I'm going to open the door to see what's going on. There's something wrong." He opened the door cautiously and could not see any reason for the Walers to be excited about inside. He pulled the door fully open, and as he and Vera were about to enter, Vera tripped and fell. He knelt to help her up, and as he looked around at the horses, he said, "Why are they doing that?"

"Geoooooorge!" she screamed, looking outside the barn.

"Heck!" he yelled as he quickly stood and started firing at the rest of the pack that decided to make their move after holding back, well camouflaged in the snow.

He was worried, for he instinctively knew that he should be out of ammo after several shots were fired off. He was too busy to do the count, and there were three beasts closing in on them that were detached from any concern of danger from the humans.

He stood and left Vera on the ground, instinctively knowing that he could fight better on his feet using his revolver as a club when out of ammo. At the same time, he knew that he had to make every shot count. He aimed at a beast that was too close for comfort and moving in fast. As he squeezed the trigger, there was nothing. "No!" he shouted as the beast kept running for him. "I'm out of ammo!" He was knocked to the ground sideways with considerable force. The impact winded him, and he had no idea what was going on. As he looked up, he caught a glimpse of Blue, the biggest of the Walers, rear at the wolf in front of him. The wolf stopped in its tracks and tried to make a hasty retreat as the other two Walers smashed through the other door that was closed, spraying them with the remnants of it. The wolf was too slow to flee after turning, and Blue closed in and inflicted a fatal stomping on it after he broke into a furious gallop.

The well-trained horses instinctively knew what to do to protect their human family. They were trained in New South Wales, Australia, hence 'Walers', for service in the Australian Imperial Forces. George helped Vera up before he quickly reloaded the seven-round chamber of his service revolver. One of the Walers, Macca, stayed with the young couple as the other two gave chase.

When Adelaide came running out with her old blunderbuss, she, too, was transformed by the spirit that watches over her and was ready to fight with bare hands, if need be. She stopped, took aim, and fired at the wolves that were just in front of the horses. She felt the kick of the old weapon. "Chert poberi, eto glupost!" (Dammit, this stupid thing) she screamed while picking herself up from the ground holding her shoulder. "Haha, that was fun!"

"Ah, Mum!" shouted George when she fired. The deafening blast from the old weapon made the young couple cower, and the two horses kept up the chase through the snow as a wolf dropped in front of them;

they were used to cannon and rifle fire in battle. He looked back at the wolf pack and thought, "Mum! Watch out for the horses!" He hurried to assist her and quickly glancing back to check on Vera.

"You should get rid of that old thing or give it to someone you don't like, Mum! You should've just let the horses finish the job.

"Are you okay?"

"What! And let them have all the fun?" She had been bogged down in a boring routine, and her soul was screaming out for the freedom and adventure she once enjoyed so must.

He screwed his face in a smile and shook his head, for part of him knew she had fun and was happy to see it, too.

The two Walers came back and received a lot of attention from a trembling Vera, but they made sure she was safe by staying close to her and constantly checking for danger.

Nikolai and Alexander came running. Alexander screamed, "Good heavens, is everyone alright?" as he studied the situation and counted the dead beasts. "How many got away?"

"Ah, two!"

"Okay, Nikolai, you stay here, George and I will track them." Having had the responsibility of a ship and his crew as a commander, Alexander knew that Nikolai would be the best man to watch the fort, as his military career as a colonel prepared him well.

When the pair took off to follow the tracks, Macca stayed at the barn doors and kept watch while everyone went to study the damaged stables. "The Walers knew I was in trouble, Dad," said Vera, and she shook her head as Nikolai put his arm around her. A tear rolled down her face.

"Here, darling, take this. You'll be okay." He gave her a revolver.

"Yes, Macca, there's a lot of love behind this mess, I know," he said to the horse and gave him a neck rub before leaving. Macca gave a neigh and nodded his head with approval.

Two hours later, Alexander and George came back. Their looks said everything. "Ah, they got up on a ridge where the horses couldn't go. They're smart," said Alexander.

"When are you two going to come to your senses and get married in Petrograd?" asked Adelaide outside the barn. George and Vera engaged in many discussions over marriage, rejecting the traditional ceremony arrangements for a typical formal occasion that was being planned for them in Petrograd. Their parents strongly opposed the low-key option the young couple wanted.

They were reluctant to tell their parents that some friends of the family were not invited because they thought they were too snobbish. Their decision was strong testament to their repudiation of snobbery and pomp and ceremony that was synonymous with nobility and royalty.

Although being close friends with the Tsar and his family, their respective families chose to ignore the harsh, heavy-handed Romanov rule that the people despised. The peasants' antipathy to the regime was growing with every blow against them, which the families were aware of, and about which no concerns were raised by them for fear of losing favour in the tsarist circle.

Adelaide said, "Vera, your friends tell me that you're a distinguished, extroverted, and strong-willed person of high moral standing, and that you're frowned upon by your peers for exemplifying the way of service. They don't know why you help the peasants. There's no gain in it. Can't you help them and accept your title as well? We love you dearly, so please allow us to give you a wedding you deserve."

Vera stopped walking with the group and gave Adelaide a look suggesting that she was not interested. She said, "I found myself eleven years ago when I saw the regime's true colours. Yes, 'Bloody Sunday' is what I'm talking about. Where was the justification in the mounted Cossack attack on those poor innocent unarmed people? The children had no chance. It was a peaceful advance on the palace, and Father Gapon was only leading them to present a petition to the Tsar, not to start a rebellion.

"They were only wanting better conditions and work

hours, and what's wrong with wanting to have the right to strike and have universal suffrage? There's nothing wrong with wanting the Tsar to stop the war with Japan. Why should they be slaughtered for doing that?"

She was starting to get passionate about the subject, and Alexander gave Adelaide a look to suggest that she should leave it alone. Vera said, "Oh, sorry, it's a sticky subject with me. It saddens me every time I think about it. Why did they have to use cannon fire on them when they were running away? It's something I'll never forget, watching the dead and dying lying in the street being trampled by those retreating.

"I know that you are friends with the Tsar and his family, but I can't associate with him. I pray that his eyes are opened to the suffering he's responsible for.

"I hope I haven't turned you against me, have I?"

"Oh, no, dear. I'm afraid you've spoken the words that I needed to hear. I'm rather ashamed of the fact that we do associate with Nicky and Alexandra, but I suppose both Alexander and I have trouble bringing ourselves to cut ties with them. We're all terribly upset with the situation that's unfolding, and we know that we could lose everything overnight."

'Bloody Sunday' triggered Vera's innate warrior that was fearlessly outspoken whenever the peasants suffered from an act of injustice by the regime. She had no need for a gun, for her mouth and her explosive passion put everyone in their place. No one was game enough to challenge her, as they knew exactly what they would be in for. She quickly gained the respect from like-minded people, of whom there were very few in the family's circle of nobility.

She grew from the experience, and the spirituality she once knew as being inactive had emerged and was guiding her in awareness. She sought answers through divination and built a shrine for prayer and guidance from Jesus. She discovered that she had an uncanny ability of prognosticating the death of a family member within days of the prediction, and she learnt to trust the strong feelings that guided her.

George, a tall, stocky, and learned gentleman whose professional demeanour was in perfect harmony with his casual lifestyle, shared Vera's philosophies. Although he was not as dedicated to the pursuit of spiritual awareness as Vera was, he showed interest in it and kept an open mind when it came to changes in his lifestyle.

Through frustration, he gained a reputation for his use of some mild colourful language, but he never got angry at anyone who pushed him too far. However, he would be very assertive with, and passionate about, his opinions, which he saw as being a more intimidating weapon at his disposal.

He was blessed with plenty of patience, and he was always caring enough to help anyone who asked for it or not. He could easily accept justified criticism, but if accused of wrongdoing, of which he had no part, one would have an experience of the real George, one that they would never forget.

When they reached the house, George said, "Vera's emotional scars are deeply rooted, and we prefer to live in the country rather than in Petrograd because the city holds too many painful memories. I know that I am expected to follow protocol and family tradition, and that your beliefs in that area are antithetical to mine, but I am sure you can break tradition. I know it's a hard thing for you both to do, considering that our ancestors had to endure the conformity of it for two thousand years, but please consider it for us."

As they entered the family room, Alexander said, "Your mother and I will give it the consideration that it deserves, soon. Okay George?"

"Yeah, sure, Dad."

Sitting around the fire, Adelaide noticed that Vera seemed to be upset with herself. She asked, "Are you okay, dear?"

"I should've listened to my feelings! They were so strong, too, telling me not to go there."

"You were lucky, dear, so don't be too hard on yourself."

"Yeah, well, I know someone's watching out for me."

"Oh, how do you get strong feelings about something like that?"

"Well, Alexander, you could call it intuition," said Vera.

"I've never experienced these things!" he said grumpily.

Adelaide said, "You'll get used to his grumpiness, dear. The uncertainty, you know, with Nicki. (Tsar) Just ignore him, it works for me." He turned his head to her and shook it.

Vera said, "My friend had the same feelings when her family tried to get her to board a steamer. She just refused to get on it. She had a terrible feeling about it.

"I had quite a tug-of-war with them, and they weren't interested in her feelings, just the cost of her education in England. But, somehow, I managed to get her to the terminal.

"They took her off punishment duties three days later when the ship they tried to force her on sank in rough seas with no survivors."

Everyone was deep in thought as they studied her words.

Adelaide said, "Vera, you've been with us for a while now, and everyone loves your baking and cooking, so grumpiness and I would love you to share the kitchen with Bruno. He said that'd be great, and we think it would be, too. Would you be interested? It'd be a good change for all of us."

Bruno, aged fifty, had been with the Zuckschwerdts for thirty years, and he was the only surviving member of his family who were all killed in the Russo-Japanese war. Alexander and Adelaide took him in and treated him like one of the family, and he spends most of his time at the estate but goes to Petrograd on occasions.

"That'd be an honour. Thanks."

Adelaide smiled, and Alexander gave a nod of approval.

From then on, friends and family looked forward to the diversity of her award-winning cuisine when they came to stay.

Three months later, Alexander was welcoming family who arrived for the planned conference. It was prompted by the dire state of the economy, which was consequential to, and further compounded by the impact of war.

Alexander's friend, Blue de Graaff, an Australian horse breeder, was invited.

The baron travelled to Australian to buy some Waler horses two years earlier. Their friendship grew over time when they both got to know one another. They found that they shared many traits, including, honesty, a non-judgmental attitude, love of adventure, horses, nature, their culinary skills in game smoking, playing chess, respect, honouring those who fell for their country in time of war, enjoying a good drop, looking after family, love of sport and fishing, and their being extroverted.

Blue loved the cool weather but would not be able to handle being snowed in for long, and Alexander preferred a warm climate but would not be able to handle a climate that was too hot.

Two

The Australian is loved by the nobles

In April, three of Vera's ten sisters were given permission to stay at the estate for a month with their governess, as that was the only way their parents, Nikolai and Natasha, could get any peace. Monica, aged sixteen, Mary, just fourteen, and Natty, almost ten, were inseparable, apart from being a hand full. They spent most of their time at the mansion or with their mother when visiting Alexandra and her children when Rasputin and Nicholas were elsewhere. They were fascinated with the country lifestyle and loved feeding the animals.

They were given the opportunity to run amuck at the estate, for Alexander and Adelaide felt sorry for them. They were discouraged by the royals at the palace to do what children normally do, and they had a strict routine that lacked sufficient fun at the mansion with no playtime in the mud. But when they were at the Zuckschwerdts, they could burn up energy that they could not in Petrograd and slept well after all the activity in the fresh air.

The dogs' barking alerted everyone to the arrival of the family at the estate in several prestige motor cars. The Australian's beaten-up motor car looked out of place as it pulled up behind the motorcade in the slate parking area that fringed the manicured gardens outside the sandstone manor house with fifty bedrooms.

Blue sat in his car thinking about his dislike for anyone who was arrogant enough to look down on commoners. As a captain in the army serving alongside British troops twenty years ago in the Second Boer War, he shared the sentiments of his men in other ranks who were reprimanded for their public mocking of British army officers for their arrogance. He, like his men, were good judges of character and gave respect to those who were worthy of it. He thought, "I wonder if I'll come across some snooty aristocrats here? Ah, well, I'll soon find out."

When he turned off the motor, a backfire from its exhaust caused a loud bang that shocked the dogs and sent them bolting and yelping with their tails between their legs as if hurt. The family stopped what they were doing and turned to Blue after they cowered in fright. "What's that!" shouted George.

"I apologise for this bucket-of-bolts car, everyone," said Blue when he got out of it.

Alexander greeted him. "Good to see you again, Blue. Did you have a good trip?"

"Yeah, mate. Hey, would you mind if I hang around for a few months? It'd be interesting to get to know this place better, and my manager is taking care of business at the station. I'll pay my way and help you out."

"Good heavens, of course you can. Go back when you want, but it could be sooner than later, I hate to say. I'll explain at the conference."

"Thanks, mate."

He nodded and said, "Come and meet the family."

"Hello, how are you, Uncle Blue? I'm Natty. Have you got a girlfriend?" she asked with a cheeky smile.

"G'day, Natty. I'm excellent, now that I've met you, and no, I don't. I've just got four grown-up kids, and you're straight to the point, aren't you?"

"Yeah, no harm in trying," she said with a smile.

As he studied Natty and her words, her sisters quickly moved in on him, too. Monica was too quick for Mary to hold his other hand and said, "She calls all our special friends aunty or uncle. Get used to it because that's what you'll be called from now on."

"Well, that's okay with me." He gave her a wink.

"Lord, they were impressed when I told them about you, hahhh, hah, poor man," said Alexander.

He chuckled. "What did you tell them?" He then

exchanged smiles with the girls.

When he was introduced to Adelaide's sister, Beth, her conversation with him was centred on her late husband while everyone listened on. She said, "I lost my husband six years ago," with a hint of emotion.

"What! You still can't find him?" he blurted out as the larrikin in him was alerted. "Ah, damn! You've done it now, drongo!" he thought as all eyes turned on Beth.

"Har, harrrrrrrrrrrrrrrr! Heavens, very funny," laughingly said Alexander.

It was a good thing everyone saw the funny side of it, including Beth, whose laughter was more subdued.

"Phew!" He shook his head and smiled.

"Yes, I'm over his passing, Blue."

"Sorry, that was very insensitive of me."

"Ah, the Walers know you're here!" said George.

Alexander said, "You can catch up with everyone when the horses are satisfied."

"Yeah, mate, they know, alright. I'd better go and make an appearance before they wreck the place." He, George, and Alexander walked to the barn with the girls in hot pursuit.

After half an hour, the horses were calm and happy to be reunited with their mate, the one who taught them everything they needed to know about war and love.

The three men and the girls made their way back to the tables that were set up beside a slate path lined with apple trees. The smell of the highly-perfumed flowers just out from the front entrance was something Blue loved, and the Russian countryside appealed to him, especially the tall trees, the green grass, and the abundance of flowers, all of which could not be found at his station in Queensland because of drought.

"Alexander tells me you play chess, Blue. Is that right?" asked Nikolai, the girls' father, who, being so devoted to the army, preferred to wear his uniform when on leave, even while considering resigning his commission due to his dismay over the suppression of his valued tactical input in the Russo-Japanese War twelve years earlier.

He was proud of his commission, but if his superiors favoured another for their obedience to their corrupt ways, there was little he could do to get the satisfaction he wanted apart from being transferred. He loved the job he was doing and wanted no other.

He gave himself a good break from the army to consider his future and preferred to stay at Alexander's estate as they are best friends.

"Yeah, mate."

"We have a few games when we're snowed in, but first we fix everything that falls apart, then practice our skills in the art of war, and keep the fires going with the wood we cut and cart. The women keep us all alive by cooking and pickling the produce from the gardens they maintain, make and mend clothes, and then they make babies to go in them.

"That's on my estate with my girls and nephews who prefer to live there. Here, I have the same routine, and Alexander prefers to have me here. I have some good men I employ to help my nephews get the job done, though."

"Mate, that's a lot of work."

"Da. (yes) There's little we can do outside when the snow is thick. We get little sun for months. I suppose you get sun in Australia all the time?"

"Yeah, mate. It's completely different to this. Sometimes we have dust storms that blow red dust from the outback all the way to New Zealand. And if you happen to be engulfed in one, the sun turns into a red ball that you can look at for as long as you like."

"It'd be great to retire in Australia, I think."

"I love it here, but I don't think I'd be able to live here for long."

When the servants brought out platters of Vera's cuisine to the outside tables with Adelaide and Vera, everyone moved in quickly to devour it.

"Struth, have those tablecloths been hand crocheted?"

"Yes, Blue," said Vera.

"How long did it take you to do that one?" he asked as he tried to fathom out the amount of patience and discipline involved in the craft.

"Months."

"Struth, I was thinking years."

"I like to cook and bake, too."

"Here, Blue, these are my favourites," said Mary as she handed him a stacked plate of assorted dishes before they made for a bench seat near a huge linden tree.

Monica seized the opportunity to sit next to Blue while Natty was at the tables.

"Here's a cup of chia, Blue," said Natty on her return, and she put it on a small table in front of him and stood next to it watching him. She intended to make a clear statement to her siblings. "I hope it's not too hot for you."

"Nah, she'll be right." He gave her a wink. She smiled.

"Sing out if you need rescuing," said Vera.

"Me, need rescuing? Struth, no!" He had a bite of her peruski pie. "Ew, they're lovely! I hope there's plenty more of these!"

"Sorry, I'm afraid they're all gone. I'll make another batch later."

"You made them?"

"Yes."

"Great." He looked at his plate to see how many were left. "Good, another two," he said to himself.

Family members came to introduce themselves to Blue while he was being spoiled by the girls, and when all introductions were over, he had a chance to enjoy the food and chat to the girls. Natty said, "Sis told me that Elizabeth loves her furniture more than she does her brother."

"Oh, is that right?" asked Blue.

"Yeah, every time we go to their mansion, she keeps watching for anyone who's walking past her prized table to make sure they don't kick it accidentally. Her brother, Alexander, knows about that and keeps teasing her.

"One time when we were talking to her, Alexander looked at us when her back was turned and gave us a smile and quickly glanced at her. He went and piled a heap of objects in his arms, and when he walked past the table with them, he cried out, 'Woooooops!' He swayed from side to side as she quickly looked around and screamed, 'Get away from my tablet!' It shocked us so much that I threw my glass of milk in the air, and it put a dent in it when it landed on it."

"Oh, what happened then?"

"We ran outside."

Mary said, "Yeah, Alexander is a really good man..."

"Elizabeth's brother?"

"Yeah, when we were over here last year, he helped us make carts so we could harness the goats and have races around the estate. It was really good fun. It's boring at our aunt's place, though, we don't have any fun at all there."

"Oh, well, we better see what we can do about that, then, hey?"

"Yeah. Will you play with us?"

"Sure will."

Monica said, "That's Vladimir over there wearing the Stetson (American hat) talking to Alexander, his brother, and that's Vladimir's wife, Fiona. Vladimir was seriously injured in the war with Japan and nearly died. It changed his life so much. Before, he was so arrogant, grumpy, and materialistic that no one liked him, but now, he delegates so that his manager can stress instead. Now, he and his family are happy spending all their time together."

"Oh, Yeah, I know how hard stress can be."

Mary said, "Adelaide is the loveliest person I've ever met, and I want her to be my mother because she spoils us. She gives us all the things that mummy won't let us have but told us not to say anything because she'll get into trouble.

"Mummy's so strict and makes us clean up after the babies all the time. She can't find a cleaner to do the job because they get sick after a day of cleaning up the nappy poo. She sits in her chair all day and shouts out orders, like we're slaves or something. She's so fat that she gets tired when she walks too long and blames it on the arthritis, she says she's got.

"Papa keeps telling me that mummy has to keep having babies until I have a brother. It seems like mummy has a baby every year. I've got ten sisters, and I'm having trouble remembering who's who, but I'd like to have a brother, too."

"Oh, Adelaide sounds like a lovely person. My sister, Louise, fits her description. You'll meet her one day. Everyone calls her Lulu."

"Hello, Blue. I'm Vladimir's brother-in-law, Mikhail. We own five warehouses in Petrograd, and that's my motor car over there," he said, pointing to the most expensive luxury car in the parking area.

"Oh, g'day, mate." Blue studied him and thought, "Oh, boy. Not one of those."

Natty's three-yeah-old sister, Josephine, went straight to Mikhail and offered him a bowl of biscuits. She said, "Hello, these are for you."

"Oh, thank you, little girl. These must be Vera's lovely biscuits I've heard so much about. Mmmm, they're lovely, but surely, they could've put them in a silver bowl…"

Vera came running and screamed, "Josephine! How many times do I have to tell you not to play with the dog's bowl!"

Mikhail's smile quickly disappeared as he turned to Vera and dropped the bowl. He then donned an unpleasant facial expression before bending over with his hand to his mouth, and then he ran away.

Vera said, "Her friend up there has been influencing her."

Blue waited for an explanation.

"Up there," she said, pointing to the heavens.

"Oh. She's got some good friends," he said, hoping he would gain the approval of her friend.

Before he sat at the fire with the family that night, everyone in the manor house heard the terrifying sound that was the dread of all dreads. "Natty's choking!" screamed Natasha as she desperately slapped her daughter's back attempting to dislodge the candy. "She's going blue! What do I do?"

"Please step aside!" asserted Blue as he got to the scene in quick time. He faced her and calmly put the open palm of his left hand around on her back, and then he put the open palm of his right hand on her stomach, fingers up. Then, with a quick thrust of his right hand into her stomach simultaneously pulling his left hand into her back, there came a pop as the candy dislodged and flew out of her mouth.

"How'd you do that?" Alexander asked, watching her gasping in precious air.

"The air in her lungs, mate. Just pushed it up against the blockage. Quick thrust, mate."

"Wow, we didn't know what to do!" George shook his head. "I can speak seven different languages! A simple technique that could save a life, and less than a minute to learn. It took me years to learn those languages."

"Where'd you learn that?" asked Alexander.

"A mate saw it done in hospital. He rode into my place when he was supposed to go somewhere else and told me about it. He said, 'I don't know why I came here,' and then he shook his head."

"Oh, isn't it alarming? The way we aristocrats can learn anything in any university that'll please us, especially in the way of anything that'll give us material gain, yet we fall short of seeking to study the one thing in life that's most important, one's health and wellbeing and the betterment of mankind. We tend to lean more toward military tactics and send our boys to the academy to learn how to kill. That's what I'm hearing all the time, anyway," said Alexander.

"That was meant to happen," said Vera in a trance-like state.

"Meant to happen? Surely, just coincidence!" argued Grandpa as everyone studied his words. He could not understand why God never helped him, so he refuses to believe.

"Well, mate, it's got me thinking. The ship I booked passage on to get here broke down. I had to get here early."

Grandpa said, "You really don't think there's a God, do you?"

"Here we go again," said Adelaide in a whisper.

"Well, mate, we're a complicated piece of equipment, and I really struggle to see how we could just develop by chance from a microorganism that washed up on a beach somewhere. The body is so complex, mate. Without a doubt, we'd have to have been created.

"All the complex parts connected to make us think, smell, hear, see, feel, and eat to help us grow. We've got legs to get around on and arms and hands to do things with. And how do you explain birth, itself? That's a miracle. That can't just happen by chance."

Everyone could see that Grandpa was starting to get passionate about the subject and that Blue was willing to pursue his argument with just as much passion, so Natasha interrupted by saying, "We're so grateful that you saved Natty's life, Blue."

Blue was Natty's hero, and she became absolutely besotted with him. She refused to leave him alone, and her sisters were growing fonder of him, too, and he, too, of them.

Dinner was served in the formal dining room on fine English bone china and crystal glassware on one of the thirty-foot-long mahogany tables beneath a huge crystal chandelier.

The dining room was only used on special occasions when family would celebrate achievements and host conferences, and the smaller informal dining room was used by family on a normal day at the estate.

Blue felt a bit out of place and said, "I could probably get used to this, but I'd hate to clean up after it, mate."

"If we were unable to afford the pleasures of employing servants, I'd hate it, too, Blue," said Alexander who was seated beside him. Monica, who was seated on the other side of him, made it quite clear that the seating arrangement she made for herself was not going to change.

"Is this grouse, mate?" asked Blue when the server brought in his main course.

"Yeah, Nikolai's cousins gave them to him to bring over. Good game meat."

"Well, this is different. At home we've got wild pig, but we've found that the kangaroo meat we give the dogs is nice and lean, so we have that, too."

"Oh?" queried Alexander.

"Herbivores, mate."

Alexander nodded.

When Alexander and Monica were eating, Blue had a chance to look around and listen to conversations between other family members, just to get an idea of their mannerisms. He was a good judge of character, and he could tell what sort of a person someone was just by listening to them talk and seeing how they act. He had dealings with many people who had different temperaments.

He made a mental assessment of everyone within his immediate radar, and of those, there were only a couple who he would consider befriending.

After dinner, the seating arrangement was made for group discussion in the family room. Another log was placed in the open fireplace beneath a huge, framed oil painting of Alexander's ancestor on his mount beside Alexander the Great. "The tradition on naming the first-born son Alexander in honour of him continued from generation to generation since June 322 B.C.," said Alexander as Blue studied the detail in the amazing rendition. "That's why there's so many Alexanders in the family."

The Australian had no idea that visitors from abroad were expected to share their life experiences. Alexander said, "Stories were told around the fire with a Vodka in the old days, but we dried out since the 'dry law' (alcohol prohibition) was brought in.

"It was only a couple of years ago many people got drunk all the time, especially at the mansion when the fighting men were on leave. A lot of good men killed themselves doing stupid stunts when they got together with plenty of Vodka.

"Their getting drunk wasn't only to escape the realities of war, which is horrific, but it was the catalyst for the temptation to participate in some risky behaviour centred on proving who was the bravest of all. My nephew is living proof of that, and it's so heartbreaking for the family to see him as a quadriplegic. A constant reminder."

"How many people get eaten by crocodiles in Australia, Blue?" asked Monica, eagerly trying to get the conversation started.

"Many, and they're smart, too. If you bed down with your swag on the riverbank, and you go to fill your billy at the same spot at the river more than twice, you're sure to get eaten. They'll know where to wait for you, and they'll give you a good old punishing 'death roll' before they lodge you under a submerged log, that's for sure."

"Wow! Can you tell us anything else?" asked George.

"Yeah, mate. I took my daughter to a beach in far

North Queensland on a holiday. She wanted to look for some seashells. Mate, you need to keep an eye on those kids, as they're so quick. I just turned my back for a few moments and heard her screaming some distance away. I took off at lightning speed and got to her when the salty…"

"Salty?"

"Saltwater crocodile, Monica. It had her in its jaws and was about to give her the roll.

"I already knew that I should attack its eyes, it's the only part of it you can do some damage to, enough for it to want to let go of something if it were hurting enough, anyway.

"I jumped on its back and wrapped my legs around it. I grabbed hold of a few teeth on its upper jaw to steady myself and went berserk on its eyeballs with my fist.

"At one stage, I thought I'd have to shoot it because it wouldn't let go. It just kept rolling us in knee-deep water, so I started thumbing and gouging instead of punching. It had enough of that and let go of her, and I jumped off it when she was free.

"Mate, it didn't like having its eyes gouged, that's for sure."

"Wow!" said George.

Blue said, "I remember hearing about a salty latching onto a woman on a beach. Her friend, another woman, tried to pull her free, but she could only watch in horror as her actions only put her friend through more agony before it pulled free of her grip and drowned her in a death roll."

"So, just like here, you need to carry a gun everywhere you go. We're definitely part of the food chain," said Nikolai.

"Oh, yeah, mate, you mean wolves and bears?"

"Da."

"Yeah, mate, and an extra pair of eyes would be handy, too."

"I noticed you were coughing when you were around Grandpa's pipe smoke. Are you an ex-smoker, Blue?" asked Adelaide.

"Yeah, but I was chain smoking then and ready to meet my maker.

"I was puffed after walking a short distance, and I'd burn my fingers every time I lit up a durry, (cigarette) or the rice paper would stick to my lips and rip the skin off them as I was taking it out of my mouth. You see, when it stuck to my lips, my fingers would slide along to the end of it and knock the burning head off onto my lap. I almost crashed the old jalopy being distracted by it.

"This went on for weeks, so I thought, 'I know someone up there's trying to tell me something, and I won't get any peace if I don't do something about it, so that's it, I'll think about it.'

"I went to my thinking spot and thrashed it out with Bazza, you know, the bloke I talk to inside my head. He said, 'Look mate, do you want to start saying your goodbyes now? Or do you want to see a lot more of your family? Try not to think too hard about it! How'd they feel if you chose to depart because you preferred your durries over them?' He was right as usual, so I gave the cigarettes their marching orders.

"Before, I was in a habit of lighting up when I finished a meal or when grabbing a beer. Getting out of that habit was an effort but sucking on a candy did the job for me."

Adelaide said, "That was very strange, do you believe that it was a spirit that did that to you?"

"I'm starting to think that way. A lot of strange things have been happening lately and a lot in the past, too, that I thought was luck."

"Oh, such as?" asked Alexander.

He had a think. "Well, mate, when I was in Honolulu, ten years ago, I watched the locals play a water game. The idea was to get on a long wooden plank in the water and paddle out to sea. They'd turn around and try to get it on a wave. When they did, they stood on it, and some of them got dumped something shocking on some huge waves.

"When I got back, I built one out of balsa wood. I gave it hardwood stringers and sealed it with linseed oil and paint. I picked a good time to try it out, though, three days after a cyclone. The waves, huh, they were monsters! And you couldn't see much in the sea spray, it was so thick.

"Don't ask me what I was thinking. One bloke

thought I was short of a few roos in the top paddock.

"I had to get through walls and walls of white water to get to the calm part where the good waves were forming, and it took about an hour to do that! When I got there, I sat on my plank exhausted and looked out to sea.

"I saw a wave and thought, 'Oh, yeah!' I had no time to catch my breath, and I paddled hard to reach it in time, thrashing when I got to the top of it, it was almost vertical. I was sure that I'd have enough time to turn the heavy thing and make a run on it, but I struggled to turn it, and when I was pointed in the right direction, I stood. No wonder that bloke thought the way he did of me. Who else would dive from the top of a fifty-foot wave into eight foot of water?

"I was like a rag doll in a washing machine when my face slammed into the sand. And my arms were useless to protect me, as they just buckled up in front of me. It was so bad that my heels pummelled the back of my head, and then I was lifted and pounded into the sand again. Do you think I could've swum to the surface? No way! It felt like I was under for a few minutes, though, but strangely enough, there was no panic.

"Then I thought, 'Relief at last,' as I felt fresh air on my face, but the heavy plank came down and kissed me right on the mouth. Pain? Nah, too quick. I was happy to latch onto it, though. It was a lifesaver. Apparently, there was quite a rip out there that could've given me a free trip to America without it.

"I threw myself on and sat spitting teeth for a while. 'I'm out of puff! Call it a day, mate,' I thought. No probs getting back to shore, the white water pushed me in.

"When my feet touched terra firma, I sat pulling loose teeth, spitting blood, and thinking, 'This really is a mug's game,' and I gave it a miss quick smart. I sure did cop a hiding while I was under, though."

"It was lucky you got out of that," said Adelaide.

"Yeah, but what are the chances of that happening, my plank coming to me when I needed it? It's just so mind-boggling."

"Well, what do you think, Vera, you seem to be deep in thought?"

"I've got to be honest with my opinions, George, some people don't believe in miracles, but that sounds very much like one to me."

"Fair dinkum? Wow! Someone sure is looking after me, and I didn't know it.

"Something else strange happened to me when I popped in on my sister at her gold mine on the Turon River, north of Bathurst. When she and I and my ten-year-old niece, Jessica, stopped to have a sticky beak at a well-used crusher, we saw a huge shale mound and decided to have a squiz. An air shaft for a gold mine.

"My sister and I stood on top of the eight-foot-high mound on one side, and Jessy stood atop it on the opposite side. We couldn't see anything, so I decided to throw a rock down to roughly gauge the depth of it by sound. It was a long way down, I tell you!

"Jessy was curious, so she slowly worked her way down the forty-five-degree slope to have a better look. On her backside, using her toes and hands to better grip the hard shale beneath the loose surface, she lost her grip and slid down to the very edge where her legs dropped over as she regained her precarious hold.

"It frightened her very much, and with a face that was a picture of horror, she calmly looked up at us. Like we were in a trance, we just stood watching like a couple of stuffed turkeys. We were in shock-still, our attention fixated as though by a spell. She bought her eyes down slowly and knew exactly what to do to get a better grip. She methodically worked her way back up, and when she reached the top, she scampered away like a frightened rabbit, greatly relieved.

"You know, had we been in a normal state of mind or being, that wouldn't have been our reaction, it would've been, 'Ahhhhhhhhh! What are you doing?' I reckon, if that were the case, she would've lost what little grip she had to startle response and fell in."

"That's strange, I wouldn't react like that," said Adelaide.

"Good heavens, strange alright. Something to think about."

"I'll run out stories if I keep going, now!"

When Blue was taken to his room, Alexander

showed him the air vent whose handle was in the down position. He said, "Don't shut it while the fire is burning, Blue. There have been several mysterious deaths among the peasants in past years. We put it down to oxygen depletion and carbon monoxide poisoning..."

"Oh, yeah, mate, I was poisoned curiously fast at home, almost blacking out. Luckily, it occurred to me that the oxygen in the room was being burnt up by the huge fire I had going in the open fireplace. No ventilation to suck the gas up through the chimney."

"Well, a lot of peasants weren't so lucky. Their fires killed them."

Three

Blue tells of his miracles while snowed-in

On the morrow, Blue awoke and opened his eyes not sure of knowing exactly where he was, stiff from the sagging wire of the brass bed and soft mattress. He said, "Oh, that's right, I'm in Russia," as he looked at the strange environment in the room.

It was a hive of activity outside, as he could hear a steam-powered circular saw cutting logs and men shouting. The roosters' crowing over the sound of trees being lopped with axes reminded him of home. He said to himself, "I better get out of bed and make an appearance, I suppose."

As soon as he drew the curtains and opened the window to look outside, he saw Monica in the chook pen waving to him. The wicker basket hanging from her arm was full of eggs. He thought to himself, "What a lovely friendly family. She seems to be a little too friendly, though. Mmmmm." He smiled, shook his head, and gave her a small wave. Her smile broadened and made him think if she was interested in him. He studied her for a few seconds with a smile to match hers before looking around at the grounds and taking in the smells and the sounds of the farm animals and birds.

He was fascinated by the manicured gardens on the estate which was surrounded by tall pine trees and a hardwood plantation where the activity was heard.

Out of the corner of his eye he noticed Monica making her way to the house and drew his attention back to her. With her eggs, she trained her eyes on him and kept them on him while smiling all the way, even when his eyes were off her. She only took her eyes off him when she tripped, which was a couple of times but made a remarkable recovery without breaking any eggs.

The environment in which he was totally engrossed provided a diversity that, had he not made the decision to leave the window, he would have been there for hours.

"Good morning, everyone."

"Good morning, Blue. I missed having a chat with you yesterday, but my name is Elizabeth, Alexander Jn. and George's sister. I always try to find an opportunity to come here because I put most of my time into keeping the family's businesses in Petrograd, and around the world, running smoothly, and I've been busy trying to settle accounts with as many of them as possible lately.

We're unsure if we'll still have them for long."

"Oh?"

"The situation in Russia."

"Oh, yeah, well, pleased to meet you, Elizabeth, and good luck with that."

"Good morning, Blue," said Monica. Still donning 'that smile,' the one she had when he first saw her from the window.

"Good morning," said Alexander. He looked at his pocket watch.

"Good morning, Blue," said Mary and Natty.

"Good morning, everyone, yeah, I slept like a baby. Must be the fresh air."

"Here, Blue, I hope I've done a good job with your breakfast," said Monica as she sat at the table opposite him after placing a plate of bacon and eggs in front of him. "I made it just for you." The cook is always obliging to share part of his kitchen with family and friends so that they can do their own thing on special occasions.

"Mmmmmmmmmmm, this makes me feel at home. Thanks, Monica," he said, not noticing how she was slumped forward with her elbows on the table and her head in her hands looking up at him with 'that look.'

Elizabeth noticed her behaviour and glanced at Alexander, returning his cheeky grin. Alexander gave a quick shake of his head.

"What else do you like apart from bacon and eggs, Blue?" asked Monica.

"Fishing, adventure, writing, growing vegetables and herbs, family, and bush furniture. Not necessarily in that order, though."

"Mmmm, that's interesting. Would you be able to help me with my art project, sometime?"

"Yeah, sure. What is it you're doing?"

"Ah…"

She had to think fast, as she had no project for him to help with. She thought that, if he offered, she could make one up to tell him straight away. She had trouble trying to think of one as he sat waiting for a reply, so she pretended to cough to give herself more time to think.

"Since when have you been interested in art, Monica?" queried Vera as she walked into the kitchen. "And what art project?"

"I've always been interested in art, but I've never mention it to anyone."

Blue looked at Monica while eating, knife and fork in hand.

Vera studied Monica who resumed concentrating on Blue.

Blue's eyes were trained on Monica as he forked more egg into his mouth.

"Come, girls! Hurry up!" asserted their governess, Helga. She was a strict forty-year-old graduate from the upper classes with a sense of humour that could be appreciated by a lump of wood or a zombie.

"Aorrrrrrr, that's not fair!" asserted Mary as she

made eye contact with Blue before she and Natty left the kitchen.

"Monica, are you coming?"

"No, Blue's teaching me today!" she said as she kept studying him.

Blue took his eyes off the governess and bought them quickly back to Monica who was smiling at him.

"Well, I'm sorry to disappoint you, but you have no say in the matter."

"Old bag!" she mumbled under her breath as she got up reluctantly to leave. Her eyes not leaving him when she left the room and walked into the door frame. "Ouch!" she cried as her hand went to her head. She turned and gave him a quick smile before he lost sight of her.

Grandpa entered and started conversation with Blue. He said, "Good morning, Blue."

"Good morning, ah..."

"Grandpa."

"Sorry for allowing my passion to have the better of me last night."

"Ah, everyone has their own feelings about certain things, Blue."

"Yeah. Do you live in Petrograd, Grandpa?"

"Yeah, I usually live in the mansion, but I've decided to stay here with my boys. Being a retired commander and missing out on a lot of family life, I thought I'd better honour that part of me before I drop the anchor.

I've never had a chance to do all the things that I wanted to do, so I'll try to get something done, now, before I go."

"All navy men in the family?"

"Yeah, for generations. When I get to play chess with you, I'll tell you all about it."

"I'll certainly look forward to that, Grandpa."

After breakfast, Blue made his way to the sawmill with Alexander, as he was interested in seeing the setup. Blue said, "They're big crosscut saws, (two-man saws) mate."

"Yeah, the men have plenty to do, so we try to make everything work in their favour. The old steam engine is struggling to keep up with the men, though.

"That's the birch plantation we manage so we can supply our customers with the best quality hardwood timber, and the left-over wood supplies us with enough firewood for two families.

"I have to employ more men to get everything done before the cold weather returns. Australia is a lot different to this place."

"Would I upset the apple cart if I were to try my hand on a crosscut saw? I've never used one before, mate."

"Sure.

"Maksim! Grab a crosscut saw and work on a log with Blue, please!"

Blue walked to the shed with him to get the saw, and he noticed that he chose a log that had a smaller diameter than the ones the other men were cutting.

Blue had spent just about every weekend at Burleigh Heads on the Gold Coast getting used to his wooden plank. The time he spent paddling the heavy board through the waves for so long gave him a strong upper body which easily matched that of a hardened sawyer, and because he gave up smoking years ago, he was a worthy competitor. He said, "What say we do this one, mate. It looks to be the same size as theirs."

Maksim was surprised by the suggestion and went to the log with Blue thinking that he would probably end up doing all the work by himself, anyway.

The other men kept working, but they knew what was going on. One of them looked at his offsider and shook his head and gave a smirk while glancing over at the Australian now and then.

Before he started, Blue took off his shirt and exposed a beefy bronzed body. He knew that the men expected little of him because of his age, but he also knew that he would be the object of curiosity when he was well and truly into it.

He and his offsider started sawing when the others started their new log, and the Russians knew that the Australian wanted a contest, so they worked at a faster tempo thinking that they would easily outdo their opposition.

Maksim was surprised when he felt that he was being pulled and pushed along, so he matched Blue's consistent effort which was not what he was used to. He started to think if he would be able to keep up with the Australian. "How old is this man?" he thought.

The other men clearly changed their attitude, and they showed some concern over whether they were going to get left behind or not.

Blue just put his head down and focussed on the job at hand and on nothing else, and, with every cut, Maksim studied Blue with a newfound respect.

Blue and Maksim finished their log and started a new one as the other men were finishing theirs.

Alexander had a smirk on his face, as he knew how fit Blue was, and he was excited to see the reaction of the men when they found out for themselves what Blue was capable of.

Alexander was unaware of Mary and Natty hiding behind a bush nearby fantasizing over Blue. They had never seen such a bronzed muscly figure before, and while they were peeping and giggling, Monica walked past them holding a jug of cold lemon water and mugs heading for the men.

"Hey!" asserted Mary as both girls ran after their sister when they spotted her.

Alexander said, "Oh, good, Monica.

"Everyone! Stop for a break!"

Blue and Maksim just finished cutting their log and reached the jug when the other men finished cutting theirs.

Monica poured a mugful of the beverage for Blue

and gave it to him, and she and her sisters stood checking him out as the others helped themselves to the drink.

"Thanks, Monica," said Blue as he took the mug from her.

"How old are you?" asked one of the men when he and his offsider approached Blue.

"Seventy, mate."

"What's your secret?"

"Battling waves in the ocean, mate. And I decided to get serious about my health and fitness after I gave up smoking. Fair dinkum, I was a real blob."

"Oh, I've never been to the ocean, and I'll never have a tan like yours."

The girls' eyes were fixed on Blue's physique, and they were totally oblivious to everything else going on around them.

Blue put his shirt on and said, "Thanks for the experience, I appreciate it."

"We should be thanking you. I'm afraid we judged you wrongly, and I for one will be looking at giving these things up if I can." He looked at his cigarette pouch he just took out of his pocket.

"Not a problem, mate. Good luck with that."

"Spasiba." (Thank you)

The girls looked to be disappointed when Blue put his shirt back on, but they were happy to walk with him, and Alexander, to the vegetable gardens where new crops were enjoying the warmer weather after snow.

Blue said, "Mate, I love gardening, and I'm taking a keen interest in pickling, too. So much stuff goes off before we can use it, and from what I gather, Vera could give me some good advice on that."

"Good heavens, yes. She's creative, and everyone loves her stuff, too. We've stuck with the basic method for so long, and talk about spicing things up, my spirits are always lifted. We grow our crops around the snow and need to preserve it to use for the months when nothing grows."

Blue was invited to sit in on the family conference that was about to get under way. The three girls sat next to him before anyone else could.

When all were seated, Alexander spoke. He said, "Well, we all know what's going on, but I'll fill Blue in on the situation, anyway, so please bear with me.

"To start with, the rouble's buying power, today, is only worth one quarter of its pre-war strength, and the woeful and worsening state of the economy, and the social mess, as you know, is consequential to the impact of war. Grain carriages railed to Petrograd have been reduced by two thirds, the cause of more and more lengthy bread queues, which, might I add, has infuriated people more than anything, especially when they suffer frostbite after waiting for hours in below-zero temperatures only to be told that there's no bread left. They'd rather starve and be warm in their homes instead of gambling on getting a loaf of bread in a queue.

"On top of that, consider the food and fuel shortages and higher prices, the exploitation of which has encouraged some very unscrupulous traders to hold back on delivery to secure a better price.

"Labour unrest, which equates to that of the abortive general strike of July 1914, a flood of workers seeking jobs in the war industry in Petrograd, and the influx of war refugees here as well, are causing huge problems that aren't being addressed.

"Nicholas has a huge dislike for unrest, but one of the worst decisions I think he's ever made, was to hand over responsibility of local government to Alexandria, for about the politics of which she knows little. Might I say, the 'German-born' Tsarina, who's allowed Rasputin to influence her in some ministerial changes, which has only given grounds for more suspicion upon the Romanovs, and about which the princes are infuriated.

"Since Nicholas assumed command of the army in 1915, he'd been bogged down in the process of fighting Germans, and since then, he's made many poor decisions. To start with, the failure to bring harmony and trust back into the management of the war effort. It's only caused anger and disgust in military hierarchy. Who in his right mind would run a war without a secretary, anyway?

"With reports of defections in many countries in Europe, along with the enormous and growing casualty rate, mutiny is becoming common place. In effect, he's put the best part of his army and just about all the peasants in Russia offside with him. The unrest that Nicholas so dislikes will come about from himself. I'm afraid that he'll ruin us all.

"It doesn't look like things are going to improve, and even if Nicholas does abdicate, would his brother want to inherit the mess? No, the Romanovs would still have a regime which the peasants despise. It's looking more and more like the Zuckschwerdt dynasty will finally be part of history, the realisation of which is a meagre prospect, but we can at least secure photographs and some riches for the sake of posterity. There's nothing else we can do about it. I had a feeling that it was a bad omen when Nicholas dropped his ring at his coronation.

"I suggest we make plans for a quick decamping now. I can see that it'd only take one incident of anger through frustration to start a rebellion, and if that were to happen, there's no guessing who the insurgents will be after. Learn from the past, we were lucky then. But Nicholas hasn't changed at all since the promises he made post 'Bloody Sunday' were broken, so we must be prepared.

"If we find ourselves in a situation where we're trapped and being searched, I think it'd be a good idea to dress down in apparel that won't be conspicuous."

"We women and girls could start sowing and stitching precious gems into our clothing in case of that happening and can't access the main stash. That way we'll at least have something to start over with," said Adelaide.

"Good idea, love, I'm sure you'll be creative about it. Put them in our boots, in our hats, and in anything else you can think of. But only put them in the clothing that we'll be wearing on the day. Also, buy some cheap jewellery to wear, no gemstones, just silver-plated chains and costume jewellery."

"We know what to do, darling."

"Any questions, then?"

"Oh, yeah! What about that black car just up the road from the textile factory? I really don't like the look of it," said George.

"Oh, yes, George. I'll wire Nicholas and try to get some assistance. That's got me worried, too, and I'm losing sleep over it.

"Blue suggested that those from either family would be welcome to stay at his Queensland station for an extended holiday while the situation in Petrograd remains tense. Let him know if you're interested. Well, that's just about it, then."

His offer was readily accepted by Nikolai and his family except Vera, Monica, and Mary. The two younger sisters put up such a fuss that there would have been no end to their complaining had they been forced to go.

They booked passage for December, and Alexander booked passage for himself, George, Blue, Vera, and the girls for Monday, February 27, 1917, (Julian calendar) four days after International Women's Day.

Grandpa and the extended Zuckschwerdt family put

their trust in the Tsar and chose to stay at the mansion to ride out the storm of unrest that was worsening.

"Blue's sitting next to me!" asserted Monica as Mary sat on the other side of him when the seating arrangements were made for group discussion after dinner.

"Our anecdotes and fairy tales have been exhausted, and we've heard them more than a hundred times over. So, Blue, you're our only hope for a good story. I hope you don't mind?" said Alexander, who would rather pass up a good game of chess to listen to Blue's adventures.

"No, I'm flattered," he said, exchanging smiles with the girls. "I want to tell you about my mate, Clive. Poor bloke, he had a rough time dealing with the separation of his fourteen-year-old daughter.

"One day he turned up at the station on his horse, Herman, smelling like a brewery. I knew that I was going to spend the afternoon talking to a brick wall when I saw the longnecks stuffed to the brim in his saddlebags. It was a good thing that Herman was well-trained and intelligent, otherwise he would've been dragged around the bush with his foot caught up in the stirrup.

"I got his beer and helped him up the stairs onto the verandah, and being a nice bloke that he is, he took his boots off before coming in. As he entered, he tripped on the raised door sill and ran down the hall to the back door where he regained his balance.

"A large flock of pink and grey galahs screeched so loud that we couldn't hear each other talk while we sat at my favourite homemade bush table on the back verandah.

"Not long before the last one, he was opening another coldie, (beer) the number of which dwindled through the one-sided chinwag (conversation) which was programmed to repeat every five minutes for the next three hours. It was like I was talking to myself like I usually do, as he talked over me and ignored my input.

"Mate! Do you think I could get him motivated to do something about contacting his daughter? No way! I had to change my strategy. I said, 'Is your getting blottoed (drunk) going to help any, mate? She is hurting, too, you know.' I had to yell at him, but that strategy was a waste of time, he wasn't interested.

"I just might have planted the seed, though, as they say. I hate to see them both suffer needlessly for a lifetime.

"After three hours, he was well and truly drunk. When he sent bottles tumbling after two flubbed attempts to get up, I said, 'You better stay the night, mate.' Nah! He wasn't going to have a bar of it. He had to go home, five miles down the track.

"As he staggered through the house, I gave some thought to the expensive ornaments, but I was more worried about him breaking his neck when he ran for the rails after stumbling down the door sill onto the verandah.

"Mate! Being slumped over the rails was just the beginning. He had to put his boots on while standing! He bent over and picked up his right foot boot and brought his matching foot to knee height, and with both hands he pulled the boot halfway onto his foot. The poor bloke was still holding the boot on his foot in that position before I helped him up. He lost his balance and slammed onto the deck on his back.

"I helped him down the stairs to the yard where he dropped his tobacco pouch when I was putting the saddlebags on Herman. The intelligent horse showed his disapproval by shaking his head.

"When he bent over to pick up the pouch, he lost his balance again and made a run for the house in a bent posture, unable to straighten up and not wanting to fall flat on his face. Like a bull charging at a red flag, the old noggin slammed into the weatherboards of the house. He stood up straight as his eyes opened wide and rolled in their sockets. He shook his head after he fell backwards into the thick grass.

"I helped him on Herman, but do you think the horse would have a bar of it? Nope! He had other ideas. The smart horse strolled under a low-lying branch of a tree nearby. He stopped when the branch knocked the poor bloke off his mount and into my waiting arms. Herman looked around, and when he saw that he was going to have another go, he moved further away. Herman could've walked him home that way, staggering behind him trying to mount him, but I made him stay the night."

"Do you know any other stories like the crocodile one?" asked Natty.

He had a think and said, "Well, the 'widow maker', having a reputation for killing a lot of people in Australia, will always be a threat that'll never be wiped out, and it's impossible to count them all, too. They always take you by surprise, and you really don't know if you're going to be killed…"

An impatient Natty asked, "Who is it, Blue?"

"I'm getting there, Natty.

"If someone stops to rest in the shade of their massive branches on a scorcher of a day, or they set up camp under them, you could just about say that their fate is unknown. You see, drought and fire affect them so much that they get stressed, and they either drop their heavy branches to save water in drought, or their weakened fire-damaged branches will drop at any time. The tree will even blow over in a storm.

"I've been on my back verandah on a fine day looking at the bush when one dropped a branch in the paddock. Mate, I'd been under that tree so many times, too. It was a huge eye-opener for me, I tell you.

"Fair dinkum, I'd been so stupid in the past, too. I camped under one of them for the night, and what happened? There was a big storm! Lucky for me nothing happened to the tree, but now when I camp out, I stay away from them and pitch the tent in open ground."

"Trees?" queried Mary.

"Too right, and rocks. When I rode into the bush near Lithgow, New South Wales, to see my mate at the coke ovens, I saw a boulder next to the road and thought, 'How'd that get there? Did it just pop up out of the ground?' It was a long way from the sandstone cliffs.

"In the dark, when I hunkered down under my oilskin on waterlogged ground from two days of steady rain, I heard a loud crack, then the crashing of rock on rock. I thought, 'Blue! You could be in big trouble, mate!'

"I stuck my head out to have a squiz but saw nothing. The boulder must've been a big one because it shook the ground something shocking.

"My horse was more scared than a frightened rabbit, so he broke free and bolted into the darkness! Yeah, my mate! Every man for himself! I thought, 'Blow this, I'm doing a runner, too.' I took off into the darkness where I thought would be the opposite direction to where it was coming from. As I ran, 'Bang!' I had no memory of anything when I woke the next morning near a tree. Yeah, a lump the size of a cricket ball on my head.

"Lots of steady rain loosened up the sandstone on the cliffs."

"There's lots to learn. I'd like to know as much as possible about Australia before I decide to go there with the others," said Adelaide.

"Hey, Blue, have you ever seen an angel?" asked Mary.

He had another think. "Well, I thought one was coming for me when I was young and staying with my parents.

"Around midnight, I was hungry and unable to sleep, so I went to the kitchen to make a sandwich, and the moment I got stuck into a jar of honey while sitting at the table, I heard my name being called in a protracted whisper several times. I turned to see what was going on, and you could say that my language was quite colourful when I saw a woman entity whose long white gown, illuminated by the bright light of the lantern on the table, was swirling around in the breeze. It gave the eerie impression of a ghost that appeared to be levitating.

"The ghost-like entity continued to whisper my name, 'Blueeeeeyyy, Blueeeeeyyy.' With its arms reaching out for me, it continued to pursue me as I fell off my chair and beat a hasty retreat on my back in a pool of honey on the floor.

"When I realised that the entity was in fact my mother, I asked her what she was doing. She said, 'I was worried that you might be sleepwalking again, so I got out of bed in my nightie and wasted no time to get to you, concerned that you might trip over something and hurt yourself. Waking you up was a worry, so I whispered your name and reached out for your arm to guide you back to bed.'"

Unfortunately, it was nearing bedtime. Blue said,

"Remember the pillow fight at my place, Alexander?"

"Ah! Alright, I'll join in this time, Blue."

"What's a pillow fight, Blue?" asked Monica as she and Mary ran up the stairs beside him with the family.

"It's an Australian thing where everyone jumps on a bed with a pillow and whacks into each other. Just having fun!"

"That sounds like fun. Are you going to join in, Dad?" asked Monica.

"So, you want to whack into me, hey? I'll probably demolish the bed."

"Goodness, Nikolai! Don't worry about the bed. I must admit I did scorn someone for putting their feet on a footrest once for fear of it getting dirty or damaged, but since then, I concluded that it was stupid of me."

"I couldn't wish for a better future father-in-law," said Vera.

"Goodness, I'm incredibly pleased about that, dear.

"We'll give the wire on this king size bed a workout. See how it goes," said Alexander as everyone followed him in the room.

When Blue got on the bed with his pillow, he was whacked in the face with the pillow Mary swung at him. He said, "Cheeky little thing!" and started on her.

George talked Vera into joining in on the action.

"What's that?" said Blue as he looked behind George after pushing the girls away.

"Ahhhhh," said George as he received a blow from

Blue.

"I can't believe you fell for that old trick, mate."

George said, "Wise guy, hey! Cop this, then!" His pillow exploded on the Australian, which sent feathers flying over everyone in the room.

"Oaaaah, poor Blue," said Monica. She sided with him and landed a couple of hard-hitting blows on his assailant.

"Hey, that's my sis!" asserted Mary as she, too, sided with the Australian when Monica was targeted.

Nikolai jumped on the bed to attack those who were attacking the girls.

Blue turned on Monica and landed a soft blow to her upper arm and waited for her response. Her dignified gaze into his eyes when she casually lifted her pillow to his arm and gently tapped him with it, was a look that surprised him, and she made no attempt to hide her actions.

Her unusual behaviour, which he picked up on straight away, was so obvious that anyone could work out what was going on. He suppressed his true emotions, which, in his lifetime, he had never experienced the likes of. Now, for the first time in his life, he was starting to see something unfold that had been missing in his life for so long. Something very new and vastly different.

"Ah!" groaned Monica as she copped a blow from George while she was studying Blue, which prompted Blue's response. Monica laid into him, too, but with a lot more vigour than she used on Blue.

"Here comes Alexander!" shouted Adelaide.

When he jumped on the edge of the mattress, George whacked him in the face as he was about to inflict Nikolai with an initiation blow. He lost his balance and fell onto Nikolai, sending the pair crashing to the floor with everyone when the wire broke.

The girls fell on top of the men, sparing them possible serious injury. Monica fell on Blue because she wanted to, and she was in no hurry to get off him. She seized the opportunity to put her arms around him and sunk her head into his neck before he attempted to get up. He wanted to put his arms around her but held back. He stayed put until the others were up, but he had a good think about Monica's behaviour before then.

"Is everyone alright?" anxiously asked Alexander through the laughter that filled the room, and he, too, started laughing when it was confirmed that everyone was.

"I can't remember when I last heard so much laughter. I don't think anyone's ever laughed so much," said Adelaide as she smiled at Blue.

When Blue got to bed that night, he struggled with the way that Monica was coming onto him. He thought, "Part of me is screaming out with joy, but the other part of me was making itself heard, too. Those old-fashioned fogies with their preconceived, old-fashioned ideals and attitudes who stamp you during conception.

"Now, I'm confused. I wonder if I should just go with my heart and see what happens? Or should I be the conformist and please everyone who may object?" After three hours of battling with his mate, the one in his head, he tried to get some sleep.

Four

Blue and the nobles help capture German spies

"Gentlemen, I wired Nicholas and alerted him to the potential threat of German spy activity in our backyard," Alexander said, addressing the men after they were summoned to his study.

"Is he doing anything about it?" asked Nikolai.

"Goodness, I'm so worried about him. He wired back a message suggesting that I was exaggerating and not to worry about it. I then wired him back to remind him of the consequences of an attack on the textile factory. I had to remind him that winter was coming up and spelt out my concerns to him, blankets, uniforms for the soldiers, and the threat of it all being disrupted by a bunch of spies.

"So often, God help me, I wanted to let him know

how I really felt about his stupidity. Fortunately, he listened to reason and obliged me by putting one counterintelligence operative and four soldiers at my disposal for a while.

"My nephews are staying at the estate with their friends for a couple of weeks before they go back to the front, so would anyone like to stay at the mansion with me to see how things unfold? It could be interesting but extremely dangerous, too."

"Yeah, I'll go, mate." Nikolai and George gave the nod, too.

At the factory, when the counterintelligence operative was due to arrive, a man whose appearance resembled that of a worker entered the office and asked to speak with Alexander.

"Yes, I'm the man you're after."

"I'm Andrei, the field operative you requested. I didn't want to blow my cover when I walked past the black car up the road to make a quick assessment of it."

"Oh! Well, you had me fooled."

"I can't wait to wash this dirt off, though, I'm not used to it.

"Well, there's two of them, and they have all the hallmarks of part of a spy ring hard at work and could only be German.

"The director was keen to have me check this one out. Naval Intelligence couldn't nab the spies who did a few black-bag jobs on them in past months."

"Yeah, they'd be dangerous, too!"

"They are, but you'll be fine if you use common sense…"

"Yeah! What's that?" Andrei looked at him for a few seconds as Alexander kept a straight face.

"I've heard that your cargo is shipped to England?"

"Indeed, the next one in three weeks."

"Good, hopefully they'll lead us to the ring the navy is after. All they know is that the intel is transmitted to a U-boat lying in wait in the Baltic.

"When we received your request, we were excited about the possibility of a connection between the two."

"Very interesting! What's your plan, then?"

"Firstly, they'll be waiting for the lorries to turn up. That'll tell them that shipment is close, and they'll be after the passage plan…."

"Good Lord, I keep that in my safe. Being a retired commander, the shipping line I deal with welcomes my passage planning. The ship's captain sticks with the usual plan unless I receive any changes, U-boats, mine fields, and stuff. I've still got friends in the navy."

"Yes, we know all about that."

Alexander had a bit of a think about that. He said, "Do you think they know what ship my goods will be on?"

"No, that's why they're out there. We know your plan is done here and handed to the ship's captain on delivery of the goods. I'm afraid it's common knowledge."

"Goodness, I'm embarrassed, now."

"Don't worry about it, war is new to us all."

"I'll need to see the captain next week when his ship docks. He has a new policy, payment a week prior to departure thanks to higher priced food and fuel."

"Is there anywhere you can go and disguise yourself as a worker or something? You'll be followed when you leave here."

"Oh! Ah, yes. I've got a friend at the Ice Truck Co. who'll oblige me."

"Is that the one just down the road, here?"

"Yes, indeed."

"I know it. Get there at ten o'clock on Wednesday morning and do your thing, and then go to my man in a grey Lesner in the side street. He'll take you to the dock and wait for you.

"In case anyone inquires, tell your friend…."

"Ah! We'll sort that out. We're old war buddies."

"Well, they'll be keen to get the plan, so make sure everyone's safe, especially your people.

"When the soldiers get here, have everyone, including them, get into a routine so the spy can get in and out without a problem.

"The job will be done at night, so keep the plan out of the safe. Give it to the captain when you see him. Put the dummy plan in the safe on the night the trucks are being loaded.

"I suggest you get your security people and soldiers

clustering around a fire at the back of the factory every night. One of my agents will be here with the soldiers until loading night."

"Oh, that sounds like fun! Life's been a bit stale in my old age. It's about time I had a bit of action."

"It's dangerous work. Are you sure you want to do this?"

"Oh, yeah! Before I retired, my cruiser was blown apart from under me when fighting the Japs. I lost one hundred men there! I'm no stranger to danger, young man."

"Please forgive me, sir, no disrespect intended."

"Well, you're right! My youth has run off with another woman…"

"Huh?"

"Everything's different now, and yes, I am feeling the pinch. I worry about it a lot, though. What I do need is a good sleep.

"What if they take off?"

"We're hoping that they'll turn up where the navy lost them last. I have men there, but we must watch how we tail them."

"Oh, they're smart."

"Give me a buzz if and when you hire workers, alright?"

"Alright, then."

"Oh, make sure everyone around the fire drum laugh loudly, and if anyone should come back to the office, tell them to make some noise. We don't want any casualties. Also, put that light over the safe and keep it on to make it easy for them to photograph the documents. Close the blinds, keep the door locked, and throw a blanket over the safe."

That night, at the mansion, Alexander discussed the day's events with the men. Nikolai and George were showing Blue around Petrograd's places of interest, and it was a good opportunity for the Australian to do some shopping.

On his arrival at the mansion, Alexander greeted them and said, "Oh, I wish I could lose the stress of all that's going on with those German spies. To think that the enemy is targeting me is frightening. From now on, I'll be carrying a gun with me, and I'll use it on anyone who threatens my family, my workers, or anything else, business and country included. Where's the Nagant, (revolver) George?"

"Yeah, that sounds like a sensible thing to do, Dad. Hang on."

George came back with it and said, "Just remember that, when you cock it, it has a hair trigger."

"Who do you think you are talking to, young man? Forty years ago, I was worried that I may have worn it out. I know this gun like I know your mother. Get me a box of cartridges, please.

"Oh, no, I forgot, Adelaide wants me to go to church tomorrow with her and the girls. I tried to get out of it but had no luck. The Nagant is coming with me, too. Being unprepared will be one's downfall.

"I wonder if those spies are outside now?" He turns out the lights and slightly draws the curtains of the window. He said, "Look at that car up the road. What do you make of that?"

Blue had a peek through the window and said, "From what I can make out, it looks a bit like there could be someone in it."

Alexander said, "Nikolai, you have good eyesight."

Nikolai had a peek and said, "A friend told me that German spies get around in those cars. Yes, that could be one."

Alexander just looked at Nikolai and said nothing.

George said, "What'd they want here?"

"Heaven above, George! They follow and spy!"

Everyone sat down and started to think hard about it, and five minutes later, Alexander went back to the window and studied the car through the curtains. He said, "I better load this thing now, just in case I have to use it in a hurry." He filled the chamber and left the gun uncocked.

Everyone was getting tired after a big day in Petrograd, and Alexander was falling asleep standing up. Blue said, "You better get some sleep, mate."

"I will probably be awake all night, as long as that car is out there."

Blue convinced Alexander to get some sleep, but he

was restless all night.

Early the next day, Alexander was up first and went straight to the window to check on the suspicious car. It was gone, but there was no way he was going to let his guard down.

The servant arrived shortly after the cook who had already prepared breakfast for the men. They sat at the dining table after breakfast discussing what they would be doing on the day. Alexander said, "Adelaide will be here soon with the girls. Are you all coming to church with me?"

They all nodded a yes and left the table to get ready.

Before Adelaide arrived, he put the revolver in his coat pocket and made sure it was properly concealed with the safety catch on.

George said, "Mum and the girls are here!"

They all piled into the luxury car with Alexander at the wheel and headed for the Orthodox Church not far away.

On their way, Alexander noticed a black car following them through the rear-view mirror. He had been stressed for days about the prospects of having a confrontation with a German spy, the realisation of which was becoming more likely when there were numerous occasions to remind him of his perceived threat. He said, "That black car behind us has been following us since we left the mansion. I hope I can stay awake long enough to get to the church, I had nothing but worry all night."

Adelaide said, "Oh, Alexander, do you really think the Germans are following us?"

"Have you lost your marbles, women? There is a war on, you know, and the textile factory is already targeted. Who knows how they operate? I'm not taking any chances!"

As they pulled up outside the church, George said, "That black car pulled up across the road, Dad."

"Do you think I'm imagining things, now, darling?"

"They are probably going to church."

"It's very unlikely, that is no coincidence."

"Oh, stop worrying about it!"

"Someone has to."

George looked over at the black car when they were being greeted by the father, and as they walked to the front pew, George said, "Two men got out of that black car and headed for the church, Dad."

"Goodness! What'd they be up to in here?"

Adelaide shook her head.

As they made themselves comfortable in the front pew, Alexander asked, "Can you see the two men from the black car, George?"

"Yeah, in the pew opposite us. They're looking at us."

"Good heavens!" He put his hand in his coat pocket and cocked his revolver, keeping his finger off the trigger and switching the safety catch off. By doing so, it gave him the added advantage of a quick shoot out, if need be, but having a hair trigger, he would have to be careful not to bump it, for it would surely release the trigger, causing the gun to shoot off a round.

When the father was well into the sermon, he was getting passionate about it, but it in no way whatsoever stopped Alexander from nodding off. Minutes later, he was getting more passionate about it, and Alexander was dead to the world, despite his brave resistance.

The father screamed, "Repent!" The startle response caused Alexander's hand to bump and release the trigger. With a loud bang, Alexander threw his arms in the air and screamed, "Shit! Shit!" and started frantically patting his coat pocket which caught on fire.

The father ducked behind the pulpit from which he was delivering his sermon as most of the congregation created a screaming stampede and made for the nearest exit. Some people kept seated and quickly scanned for suspicious activity and some looked at Alexander.

The events in the past were constant reminders that the church and its parishioners were not exempt from the Tsar's heavy-handed rule, and they knew that retribution was something that the Tsar would be capable of dishing out. The father thought that the time had come to receive it, and not being sure after hearing just one shot, he popped his head up from behind the pulpit with his eyes opened wide and ready to duck again.

Being closest to the gun going off, the family members, and Blue, turned to Alexander after cowering in shock.

In the confusion and screaming, Alexander said, "I think we should go now."

They got up to leave while people were still running out, and George noticed that the two men he suspected of being spies were not there.

Adelaide and the girls stayed at the mansion that night. After dinner, when the servants and the cook left, Adelaide said, "Well, Alexander, what am I going to do with you?"

"Give me a bottle of Vodka?"

"You may think this is funny, but it's deadly serious! What if someone worked it out that you were responsible for firing that gun, and word got around that you are the most likely culprit? Embarrassment would prevent me from ever going back there. What if something terrible happened?"

Blue was hiding his face and doing his best not to laugh, but he had to leave in a hurry before he screamed with laughter.

Nikolai and George had to join him because they, too, were doing a poor job of suppressing their emotions.

"Can you stop nagging and get something to put on this powder burn I'm suffering from? Have you no compassion, woman?"

"Yes, but not for you! It's a good thing no one was shot."

Adelaide and the girls went back to the estate the next day, and the men spent a couple of days at the factory with the agent rehearsing their plan.

Two weeks later, Alexander drove to the Ice Truck Co. factory to disguise himself before going to see the ship's captain. As thought, the spooks followed him there where one of Andrei's men was staked out.

Alexander's friend, Ugoofoff, greeted him and said, "My old friend, it's been a while. I got your wire. About time we got a bit of action around here, for that stupid kid in me kept complaining all the time.

"Are we allowed to kill them?"

"Good Lord, no!"

"Ohhhh, what a shame. But I suppose we can have a little fun with them, yes?"

"Of course. See that black car out there…?"

"Don't tell me that's a spy, is it? He looks familiar to me."

"That's a spy, alright!" said Alexander.

"It doesn't look like he's done a hard day's work in all his life. Huh!"

"Shit, here he comes! What do we do?"

"Give me your hat and coat, quick!"

"Shit, no, I've turned the sleeves inside out and can't get them off!"

"Just get it off, quick!"

"Heavens above! Ewwwww," he grunted as he fell backwards on the wet floor.

"Sorry, Alexander. Well, at least I got one sleeve free.

"Urei, help us here, quick!"

Alexander accidently bumped a box which had a cricket bat on it. Ugoofoff said,

"Watch out for that bat!"

"I got it. It was about to fall on your head, Alexander."

"Yes, I know."

Alexander was struggling on the wet floor with his ripped coat. Ugoofoff was pulling at the coat sleeve trying to yank it free, and Urei was standing over Alexander holding a cricket bat.

When the man walked in through the double door entrance, the men on the floor froze and turned to look at the man who just walked in, thinking he was a spy.

"Ahhhh, ah, ah, I didn't see anything, I swear, I didn't see anything," he said before he turned around and ran to his car across the road. He cranked the engine while looking back at them and sped off down the road.

The men just looked at each other. Alexander was helped up before they cautiously looked through the window.

"Oops, look over there. A black car over there, and that looks more like a German spy sitting in it, to me," said Ugoofoff.

"Oh, get this coat off." They hurried towards the lunchroom.

"Urei, stay here in case he comes over. Going by the way he was looking over here, he just might suspect something."

Urei said, "Ahhhh, I know who it was who walked in

the door on us! I knew I seen him before."

"Yeah, I remember, too. Popoff, I wonder if he'll ever come back? He's our best customer.

"Here, get into these clothes, Alexander.

"If anyone asks, Urei, tell them I'm busy with an important customer."

He changed clothes, shirt and all, before ducking out the side entrance where he got into the agent's car. He was holding a handkerchief to his face and was bent over, using a walking stick.

When he met the ship's captain at the harbour, he explained the reason for the disguise and warned him of the situation before taking care of business, drilling him on the precautions that he should take to avoid any trouble.

Three days before the lorries arrived at the factory, one spy disappeared from the car.

When Alexander told the agent that he'd just hired some men for loading, the agent was quick to tell him that the spy would more than likely be among those men, just what Alexander suspected, too.

"Do you know who the owners of these cars are, Alexander?"

"Yes."

"We can't afford to lose track of the spy in the car. It's a pity we haven't got a description of the one you hired, but we'll see him when he's done the job."

"I've got a couple of men you can use. My son,

George, and a friend, Blue."

"Oh, good, when the spies have done the job, and they both leave, the three of us will tail them. I'll be behind Blue and George, and whoever is behind them will have to turn off after five minutes so as not to arouse suspicion but come back behind me when I pass. The next one behind them will do the same, and I'll take over from there.

"There's a chance that they may each take off in separate cars from the factory, so we'll have to be ready to tail two cars. In that case, Blue and I will stick with the one who comes out of the factory."

"We're here, on this map of Petrograd."

"Oh, good. If anyone should lose them, proceed to the harbour. I'll be waiting for them there where my men are stationed, ah, here." He points to the position on the map.

"That seems to be straight forward."

"The trouble we go to is well worth it, but as you say, they are smart.

"Let's hope it's quiet on the streets that late at night."

"Ah, goodness, I hope it is."

On the night when the lorries were loaded, Alexander made sure that the new men heard him tell his secretary that he'd just completed the passage plan and will be leaving it in the safe overnight.

When all the workers finished loading the lorries, the foreman and the agent started conducting a secret headcount while inconspicuously hiding behind some timber opposite the factory's main entrance. The foreman confirmed that one of the new workers was unaccounted for when the rest of the workers had left.

The agent was concerned when the black car was nowhere to be seen. It was thought that it would be too far for someone to ride a bike to the harbour but was considered a possibility. All motor cars in the immediate vicinity were checked before the spy left the factory.

Alexander wanted to give the spy plenty of time to break into the safe, so he stayed with the soldiers and the security team for a good half hour before going back to the office. Upon opening the safe when he did go back, he noticed that the manila envelope containing the dummy plan was not exactly in the same position as it was when he placed it in there.

When the suspect emerged from the factory, the agent kept his distance and followed him in his car to a different car in which his comrade was waiting. He waved to Blue who was following well back to come when they drove off away from him. Fortunately, they drove off in the direction of the harbour before going around the block, and they were successfully tailed all the way to Petrograd Harbour as planned.

Tailing them seemed to have been working quite well, but when Andrei's men took over the tail at the harbour, the spies disappeared. Their car was found abandoned, and there was concern of failure, but the agent was determined not to let the fugitives get away, so he got his men to inconspicuously search the immediate area on foot. They were told to keep behind the bushes and make their way to the other agents who were already staked out.

It was a matter of waiting, watching, and thinking, now.

Ten minutes had passed, and the agent was getting anxious, but one of his men ran in front behind Andrei and informed him of a sighting.

He drove to a lorry in which his men communicated through a special kerosene lamp signalling apparatus in the back that was aimed at a destroyer, the command post for the naval intelligence side of the operation.

The contact source was identified as being an old sailing vessel that had just come in and was seen to have flashing lights coming from it.

The information Andrei provided was signalled and the navy dispatched the longboats carrying several navy infantry personnel (marines) shortly after two men had been seen getting into a rowboat and started rowing toward the dock where the men were.

Andrei's men moved in quickly to block all escape routes and waited for the boat to reach the dock from the ship. As soon as the incriminating evidence was handed over to their comrades on the rowboat and were out of sight as they rowed away, the two were apprehended as they left the dock. Without a shot being fired, they were bound and gagged before they were taken away.

The navy destroyer was in a good position for its covert operation to be initiated. The longboats view from the dock was obstructed by the sailing vessel, so the men in the rowboat were unaware of anything going on when they were returning. The navy infantry personnel professionally boarded the sailing vessel without making a noise as its crew watched the men rowing back. As soon as the two men boarded the vessel with the incriminating evidence, they were quickly apprehended and were prevented from disposing of it.

Andrei had done his job, and the navy had shut down the German spy ring that was responsible for transmitting highly classified Intel to their U-boat comrades.

Navy destroyers were sent to strategic locations in the Baltic where U-boats were likely to be lying in wait to ambush a steamer.

Five

Vera sought solace from her dad over her rape

The weather was getting cooler, and the men gave their best effort to finish cutting and splitting the felled timber that had been drying out for more than five years. They had to ensure an adequate supply for heating and cooking during winter. They always allowed for an extra month's supply for bad weather, as they had a dislike for cutting wood in below-zero temperatures.

It was the time of the year when the women and children were busy pickling the fruit and vegetables before it spoiled, but, despite their tight schedules, Vera and her father found the time to talk at night, sitting around a cosy fire outside. It was the only opportunity they had to really get to know one another better, as Nikolai's priorities had been determined by the army in the past.

Time spent with his daughters he knew had to be quality time. There were many times when he wanted to leave the army and just be a father. He had always seen younger men than himself killed in war, leaving behind children who had only seen their father once or twice.

One night when they were sitting around the fire outside in the early hours of the morning, Vera hit her father with a bombshell. "Papa, our babysitter raped me when I was five years old ...."

"What! Sergey raped you?"

"Yes, I wasn't going to tell you because I didn't know what you'd do. Cause trouble or not..."

"No! I'd never cause trouble for you, my poor baby. Tell me about it."

"It happened at the mansion when he came to babysit us. I hate to go into details. It was so horrible."

"How long did that go on for?"

"Months and months, that's why I stayed with Gregorio until I met George.

"I was a real mess. It would've been worse without him. He carried me through it all."

"Did you tell your mother?"

"No, she probably would've thought I was lying."

"How can he go about life like it never happened when I see him? Does he think I was too young to remember it or something?"

"He obviously thinks you're not going to do anything about it."

"Has he got a conscience, Papa?"

"I really don't know, only an animal could do something like that.

"I'm so sorry, darling, I feel that I've let you down by not being there for you when you needed me."

"It's not your fault. Where was mum?"

"No doubt the pain never goes away."

"It's always there, but when I have a bath or see a boy and girl playing, I have a deep hurt attack and cry till I can't cry anymore tears. There's something that has helped me a lot, though. I can still remember the faces of the 'Bloody Sunday' children. At least I'm still alive and got all my limbs. I have no problem compared to most, and all my hurts pale in importance.

"The only psychotherapy I could find in hospital was limited to encouragement and reassurance.

"Gregorio tried to help me understand the meaning of life so that I can better cope. He said, 'All people are here to learn, and it doesn't stop with just one lifetime.' He said, 'If the soul doesn't learn in one, it'll be reincarnated into another, and another, and the lesson will get harder each time until their soul screams,' and...."

"Karma. Someone told me about it. Do good or bad and get rewards or retribution. Do you really believe that?"

"Yeah, you've got to be responsible for your actions. 'Let go and let God' is what I must do. I'm concentrating on that. I do pray that he learns his lessons, and I'm ready to forgive him, but he'd be lost if no one prayed for him.

"I always remember Jesus wanting us to love our enemies but often wondered why we should. Maybe it's because we, ourselves, would hate to be stoned to death for an indiscretion that was a part of our learning process. I suppose Jesus wants us to be patient with people because they, like us, are basically decent people, and they too, need the learning challenges that we no doubt had to face in a past life ourselves."

"Are you going soft on him?"

"Not really. Since I prayed to Jesus to help me with compassion, he delivered."

"I'm sorry, but I'll have to give him the glove, and until the day the dual takes place, he's fired, and he won't be allowed to visit anymore."

"No, Papa, don't kill him! Please let me do it my way, I'm just not ready for more complications. I just want to forget it all.

"If I were to expose him for what he did, the whole family, including his wife, would probably leave him, and then the suffering would branch out in all directions. No one in his family would want him around the children, and the consequences of that alone would be incalculable. Just imagine, he wouldn't be able to attend family functions, and he'd be broken-hearted and suffering in his lonely existence. Isn't that punishment enough? You don't have to kill him."

"Sorry, darling, that's the way it goes."

"His materialistic aunt would dump him like she would a bucket of horse manure because she's so judgmental and unforgiving, and compassion is something she has never had. His other scandalmonger aunt would make sure that the indiscretion would reach everyone's ears. Can't you just let it go at that?"

"I'd do anything for you, but you know the family's code of conduct. An attack on any member of the family is an attack on me, personally, and I've got to honour the code. He knows that, too. It's a wonder he's still here and hasn't taken off."

"G'day, you two," said Blue as he and Monica came out from the house at daybreak.

"Have you been out here all night?" asked Monica.

"Yeah, I've done something that I've neglected to do for the past seventeen years."

"Oh?" queried Blue.

"Yeah, take an interest in my girls. Well, at least one now, and I'll work on the rest some other time."

"Yeah, mate, that's important. My father kept us from seeing pop because he was treated badly when he was a kid. He was a stewing pot of hatred.

"He wanted to do a runner, but he knew he'd be strapped to within an inch of his life if he did.

"He left home when he was old enough to fend for himself and never went back. I suppose pop was too depressed to be compassionate and couldn't see the damage he was doing. He realised it later, though.

"I can understand how he felt, though. But through his hatred for pop, he failed to see the bigger picture, the 'why' behind it all.

"Mate, it hurts when I think of it. Poor pop, he wanted to see us when it was too late. I hope future generations are spared the pain of that."

Blue spoke no more, and he shook his head as he was overwhelmed with emotion.

Monica donned a sad face before Nikolai walked up to him and put his hand on his shoulder. Monica put her hand on his other shoulder to comfort him. He said, "Good mates."

"It's good to see you're human, too. Come Vera."

That day Nikolai approached Sergey at the family mansion and said, "I was just informed by Vera of an indiscretion on your part when she was five, and her assertions that your duty of care was ignored and replaced with a duty of lust leaves me with only one option, and you know what that is. Before I serve you with it, I will seek and peruse your written response in your defence of it.

"I will expect a reply from you by 8am tomorrow, upon which time, if you have decided not to leave the country, I will serve you with the challenge in accordance with the rules from the family code of conduct. You and the witnesses of your choice, and I and those of mine, will assemble in the woods at the Petrograd firing range on Tuesday next week at noon."

"Firstly, sir, I admit to being responsible for the indiscretion that no doubt has caused so much suffering and pain for Vera. God knows that the punishment I put myself through about this has been severe, and I've already decided to repent and beg Vera's forgiveness.

"I'm not about to leave the country like an irresponsible coward. I've learned my lesson, and there's no doubt that your experience will finish me off, but at least I will have been true to myself knowing that I accepted responsibility for my actions and paid the price. I'll tell you here and now that I will be there."

Notwithstanding he was without title, Sergey's social status in the upper classes bordered on a high level of respect, but now, there was potential for adverse circumstances to arise that could ruin him.

Nikolai said nothing for a moment, and then he nodded and left.

Nikolai's life was in the process of going through a spiritual transformation, a new phase where healing was taking place on his past mistakes, bad habits, and wrongdoing. He was guided to the people who were sent to help, but It was particularly hard for him, being a baron and a colonel, to make a major 'about turn' when his whole psyche had been programmed and cemented in the familiarity of nobility and its practices. Progress was being made, though, and he could see it, too. He was willing to change for the better, deep down.

On the day of the dual, all parties arrived, and in accordance with the agreed-upon rules, pistols were to be used and were handed out for both parties to inspect.

Nikolai said, "Well, Sergey, you have demonstrated your willingness to risk your life for your new-found principles, and I admire you for that. Are you ready to change your mind?"

"No, but I reiterate, I have decided to repent." He turned to Vera who was present and said, "Please forgive me, Vera."

Vera's emotions overwhelmed her, and she ran away.

Sergey said, "I accept my fate, and I'm ready now for what is to be. I'm not going to dishonour myself by withdrawing now."

They followed directives for the procedure and engaged in the initial steps, and when the correct number of paces were executed, they both turned quickly. No shots were fired, and both men stood aiming their pistols at one other in a catatonic-like state, as if both men were disabled by a higher power which was in full control of their actions. They were subjected to the spell for some time while onlookers were bewildered and anxiously waiting. They were both alert but unable to move.

Nikolai noticed that Sergey moved his pistol slightly to one side before the ball exploded from it with a loud bang. Nikolai blinked when a shot rang out and was nicked in the ear by the ball. Sergey lowered his pistol and waited for Nikolai's response.

Nikolai was bewildered by the spell, but he knew that it would be a disgrace if he were to kill Sergey now, knowing that it was more than likely that Sergey spared him. It would haunt him for the rest of his life. The spell lifted and motor function returned, and he paused to think while aiming at his head before he moved his pistol slightly to one side and shot at Sergey, nicking him in the ear, and then he lowered his pistol.

Vera, who was far from the action, heard the first shot ring out and burst out crying, thinking that Sergey had no chance at all and was killed before he could fire his pistol. When she heard the second shot, she looked over and ran to see the outcome.

Nikolai looked at Sergey and said, "My teacher had everything to do with this." He then walked off deep in thought, and when Vera ran to him looking at Sergey, Nikolai said, "How did you do that? I wanted to kill him."

"What?"

"Disable me. I was trying to shoot, but there was no way I could move, but then I saw him move, and I thought my time was up."

"God answers my prayers in some pretty strange ways, but I must confess that this is the first time I had some doubt about the outcome. I'll just have to try harder to pray and trust next time."

"I just can't believe that.

"Well, today is a big day, and if we want to go to Australia, we'll have to start packing, soon," he said shaking his head.

Six

A bear hunt gone wrong with a pack of wolves

George and Vera both agreed to get married in Australia, which was something that they really wanted, so they put their marriage plans on hold until they were with everyone there in February.

Germany was building more submarines to bolster her long-range U-boat fleet while debating the restoration of her use of unrestricted submarine warfare. That was initiative enough for the family to ward off the danger of procrastination and leave as soon as possible. The way it was, the situation could change at any time.

The only reassurance that Nikolai and his family had for a safe voyage was knowing that Germany was against antagonising America, provoking her into severing diplomatic relations by sinking passenger ships that would result in American casualties.

Nikolai could not pray and not worry or trust, which he knew was an insult to the entity he prayed to because Vera told him many times, but It was hard for anyone to pray, and trust.

Blue had made prior arrangements for the family. He knew that they would be safe, but he really wanted to go with them.

There were a lot of sad faces that night as everyone sat around the fire discussing the latest news on German U-boat activity in the war zone around the British Isles. Their efforts to seek reassurance carried a hint of fear which Vera picked up on straight away, and she made everyone aware of the danger of it and tried to help them be positive.

Blue saw the need for them to train their thoughts in other areas, suggesting that he share a funny story with them. As soon as he was about to open his mouth, the dogs started barking, and the horses started demolishing the stables again. Everyone knew by the intensity of the commotion that it could only be a bear or a pack of wolves.

Like it was second nature to everyone, including Blue, they knew their jobs and hastened into action. The Orloff family, like most who had country estates fringed by the wild, drilled their young the same way a military sergeant would a recruit.

Alexander said, "Oh, here we go again! Grab your rifle, Blue. Business as usual." The men ran upstairs for a vantage point in the bedroom adjoining the barn, the obvious target for wild game.

George got to the window first. "Bear! Our old troublemaker friend, again!"

"There's two of them! The other one's over there!" shouted Alexander.

"I'll just have a sticky beak, mate. You do your thing."

"I'll take the one at the barn door, Dad." He put the magazine in his 303 rifle and chambered a round before firmly gripping it against the window frame to steady it, and he said, "Sing out when you're ready, Dad."

On the count, they both shot at their target.

The beast at the door was standing on its hind legs pushing against it, but it dropped down on all fours in a split second before George fired. "He's down, but have I killed him?"

"Oh, no! Mine went down, but he got up and took off.

"I should've let you have a go, Blue."

They ran downstairs to grab their coats and prepare for a hunt.

"Give me strength! Girls, you know the drill, fire off two rounds of the revolver if there's any trouble."

As the men ran out and headed for the barn, Vera had a terrible feeling about the situation and grabbed her coat before giving chase.

They reached the barn and Alexander said, "He looks dead to me!" They kept their distance, studying the beast in the blood-stained snow.

Blue chambered a round in his 303, ready to make sure the beast was finished.

"Wait, be careful! Something's not right!" screamed Vera.

Blue kept his rifle trained on the bear as he and the others turned to see what she was screaming at.

"Ahhhhhhhhhhhhh! Look out!" The bear jumped up and made a run at George when they took their eyes off it.

"Ah!" George shouted as he was knocked down by a powerful blow from its paw, sending his rifle flying.

Vera screamed, "Oh, no! What have I done?" She froze and looked on in horror.

Blue quickly turned and brought his rifle around to aim at its largest body mass. He squeezed the trigger and shot it in the stomach before it had a chance to stomp on George.

"Lord, help us!"

The beast turned on Blue and showed no sign of slowing. His standing his ground and chambering another round with the beast bearing down on him was a huge concern for Alexander who could only watch.

After a quick bolt action to reload, he quickly brought his rifle up and took aim between its eyes. As a huge paw was about to come down on him, he squeezed the trigger, taking its face off.

George was in shock by the suddenness of the event

and was slow to react when the bear fell backwards onto him. "Ahhhh! Get him off!"

Vera was stopped when she ran to help George. "Ah, girl, stay back!" said Alexander.

"Mate! He should be dead, now, surely!" He chambered another round and moved around so that the finishing shot would miss George and the others. He put the rifle barrel to its head which was resting on George's stomach and said, "Just to make sure, mate." He put a big hole in its head, and when they saw that it was safe, the others came to help free him.

"Any broken bones, mate?"

"I don't know!" He checked himself. "No, I'm fine."

"I'm so sorry! How silly of me!"

"Everything's alright, now, Vera.

"We better track the one I shot," said Alexander.

"Will you be up to it, mate?"

"Heck, yeah! Nothing's going to stop me."

The early cold front dumped about an inch of snow, and the fresh blood in it alongside the tracks told them that the bear was in a critical state.

"Okay, Bloodymere, you've got work to do!" said Alexander.

The bloodhound strained on its lead, ever pulling Alexander along after he slung the rifle over his shoulder to manage him with both hands.

After following the tracks for a good thirty minutes, the dog responded.

"Bloodymere's on to something. Keep your eyes peeled!"

"There he is!" shouted George.

"Lord, the wolves want him, too! You better shoot him, George."

When he shot, the branch that the beast was scaling snapped, sending the massive carnivore into the snow. The wolves surrounded it and attacked from all angles.

The men stood and watched, but when the bear decided to make a run for it in their direction, they turned and ran. "Aowwwwwwww! Shit, George!" They ran into each other and bumped heads, but Blue ran the other way.

"Oh!"

"What is it, Dad?"

"Nothing!" There was no way he was going to tell him that he just had a huge wet fart.

He dropped the dog's leash to grip the rifle with both hands as he leapt through the snow saying, "Oh, I'm too old for this stuff!"

The dog left them to fend for themselves and took off ahead of George who tripped and fell. "Look! Get under that fallen tree!" shouted Alexander.

He and Blue helped George up.

"Owwwwwhhhh, mate! Something must have died in here. Smells like rotten prawns in a dead dingo's carcass!"

Alexander's eyes rolled in their sockets as he shook

his head.

The cover under the fallen tree provided protection from all angles except from the front, the only way for the bear to clamber in. "Get out! Quick!" shouted George as the bear was heading for them.

"Mate, the wolves!"

"Oh, no!" shouted Alexander.

"Get out, mate!" They quickly clambered out of the tree-covered trench.

"Struth!" The wildlife rushed past them.

Blue helped Alexander away from the entrance. If they were any closer to the wildlife, they would be part of the action.

"Surprise, surprise, Dad! Bloodymere's tracks."

"Phew, that's fowl, something else must have died around here, too, mate."

"For crying out loud! It's me!"

"Oh."

"What'd you have for dinner, Dad?"

"George, I'm in no mood for your smart remarks. This is serious!"

"They're giving the old boy a run for his money, mate. They've forgotten about us."

"Oh, I'm out of breath. Keep whistling, he's not that far away," said Alexander.

"Hear that, mate?"

"That'd be right! There he is, watching from a distance," said George.

"Lord, no! Bad weather! Keep sniffing, Bloodymere!"

"I'm done, too much snow on the tracks."

"Don't be so negative, George!"

"Look, mate! We can regroup over there!"

"I'll stay with the dog," said George.

"Mate, ah, I'll stay with him, too, he might find the trail."

"For Pete's sake! I can't help it!

"Going by the sun, home should be over there, somewhere," said Alexander.

"Heck, I don't know! We'll do a couple of sweeps with the dog. Got to do something."

A few minutes later. "Oh, good! Bloodymere's onto something," said Blue.

"Thank goodness! Keep sniffing!"

All three suffered anxiety attacks whenever the dog stopped and sniffed back and forth and side to side. "She's easing up now, mate. He's got a good whiff of it now."

Finally, they made it back to the estate where everyone was waiting at the barn doors, armed and ready for any further unexpected surprises.

George went straight to Vera who showed great joy to have him back in one piece. She said, "We were so worried about you. What's that foul stench, eeerrrrrrrr-rkkkkkkk! I've got to get out of here."

Alexander left the group with his head down. As George looked around at him, he said to Vera, "He had a huge runny-fart accident when we ran into each other. I'll tell you later."

"I'm so sorry, I feel like such an idiot! And screaming out to you before. What's wrong with me?" she said as she shook her head.

"Nothing is!"

"The Walers almost demolished the stables again, Blue," said Monica as everyone went to see them.

Monica was patting Sheila who was on her left, and Blue was giving Macca, who was on his right, a neck scratch, while Blue, the other Waler in the middle, turned his head from side to side wanting a scratch, too. Adelaide, Vera, George, Mary, and Grandpa were standing facing the horses and talked with Blue and Monica for a good fifteen minutes, after which time George and Vera decided to go back to the house.

Adelaide decided to go, too, and when she got to the doors, she called out, "Are you coming Grandpa and Mary?"

"No, I'll stay and talk to Blue for a while," said Mary.

"I'll stay for a while, too," said Grandpa.

"Grandpa!" called Adelaide.

"What?" he asked, trying to work out what she wanted. And he only realised when she screwed her face and gestured for him to come.

"Oh, Mary, can you come and give me a hand with something?"

"I want to stay here and talk to Blue for a while,

Grandpa, I'll help you later."

Grandpa turned to Adelaide and screwed his face with raised eyebrows and shrugged his shoulders before walking out. He and Adelaide then went to the house.

Five minutes later, Adelaide called out, "Mary! Vera is making gingerbread men to bake soon. Do you want to come and help?"

"Okay, I'm coming!"

"Oh, yes, I love Vera's gingerbread men, I'm coming, too," said Blue as he turned to Monica to ask her if she was going.

Blue had his back to Macca, but the clever Waler put his nose against his back and nudged him toward Monica. "Ewww, sorry, Monica," he said as he was flung into her arms. They both stood, arm in arm, looking into each other's eyes saying nothing. He could see that she wanted to kiss him, and all three Walers neighed and nodded their approval.

"Ahhhhhh, sorry, Monica, I can't kiss you."

Monica just looked at him with a sad face.

The horses shook their head with disapproval before Macca nudged him gently again.

They looked into each other's eyes and smiles were exchanged before he let go of the embrace. "Cheeky horse, you," he said when he turned to Macca, who answered back with a nod and a neigh. "I'd like to go back to the house to clean up." She was reluctant to go, but she gave him a short smile before making a move toward the doors with him. He gave her a big smile which broadened hers.

When they reached the doors, Blue said, "It's not that I'm not interested in you."

Those words gave her something to think about, and she walked back to the house with him looking at the ground, and back at him, deep in thought.

She had again impacted on his ability to maintain rational thinking, but now, he had some serious thinking to do. He needed time alone to think about it. For now, he just needed to try to concentrate on something else. He challenged Grandpa to a game of chess. He told himself, "Think about how you're going to deal with it in bed tonight, okay!"

"Well, Blue, I'll take your knight and see what you're up to."

"Ah, no, mate, I can't think at all."

"Someone has taken more than a keen interest in you."

"Yeah, mate, and I don't know how to deal with it."

"There's nothing you can do, she's like a bloodhound. Once she's got her mind set on something, that's it.

"We use her to see how she reacts to certain people, and we know who to avoid or befriend. Many have fooled me, but no one can put it over her.

"Nikolai knows she dotes on you, and he's okay with that, too. There are not too many good men in aristocracy, I'm afraid. All the good ones are snapped up pretty quick."

Blue shook his head and said, "Fair dinkum?"

He looked around, and as he thought, she was sitting down looking in his direction. He thought, "I wonder if she'd still feel the same way about me when she's eighteen? I don't know, but I'm not going to encourage her."

She watched him for three hours through the four games he lost.

After the games, he congratulated the baron and sat back in his chair to talk with him. Monica came over with two cups of hot chocolate for the pair and asked, "Do you mind if I join you?"

"No, sit. I was just telling Blue of my war days as a commander. Now he's well informed. Yes, the navy's been in our blood for centuries and always will be."

"Mate, you should write a book."

"Net, (no) Blue, I want to forget about it all."

"Something for future generations, mate. They'd be proud to have it to study or to be inspired by, and you could help so many people, too."

Grandpa just pondered over it.

Alexander asked, "Have you started without us?" The family moved to Grandpa's circle.

When everyone was settled, a caller arrived. Adelaide called, "Vera, dear, there's a letter for you!"

"For me?"

"Yeah, dear, come on, open it up!" she asserted.

"It might be personal!" said Alexander.

"No, it's from Elizabeth. She says a friend's mother is having a lot of trouble with a suitor. He refuses to give up on her, even after she told him to his face that he was obnoxious and wants him to leave her alone. She says here that he's a very arrogant womanizer and a disgusting gold digger. How can we get rid of him?"

"Ah, how I hate them!" said Alexander.

Vera looked at Adelaide with raised eyebrows and a cheeky smile.

"What?"

"You're bound to find out sooner or later."

"Hello, what've you done?"

"Well, you know that disgusting individual who was after Beth three years ago, the one who kept forcing himself on her?"

"Oh, Beth told me. What about him?"

"Well, his giving up on Beth had nothing to do with his being bored with her."

"Really?"

"My friend, Helga, and I, devised a plan and took it to your textile factory, Alexander, to seek the help of your carpenter, Boris."

"Oh, Boris. He's a giant! A scruffy and scary looking fellow but a decent lad."

"Anyway, we told him of our plan, and he was excited about wanting to help. We gave him makeup to play around with, and when the photographer turned up, he was a bit hesitant about being in his company.

"At that stage, he was topless and wearing baggy britches and knee-high boots. We glued hair all over his upper body, arms and all, even gave him bushy eyebrows. No work was done to his face, he was scary enough, but we gave him a nice shade of lipstick.

"He posed with his legs apart and held a bottle of Vodka in his left hand, and we got him to hold a huge sword high in his right hand. He had a couple of missing teeth, so he gave a big smile. And with his eyes opened wide, he was a sight that would frighten the toughest of men.

"When we got the photograph, Helga and I fabricated a letter so that we could send the lot to his place. We wrote in the letter, 'Hello, Gagarin, my friend. I see you around many times, and me like you. Hope we meet soon, be good friends, da? You make Samba happy, you good for Samba. Do many things together, da?'

"That was the first of two letters..."

"That explains why he was so nervous when he was at Beth's place. She said he'd peep through the window and look around, and he'd sit and bite his nails while deep in thought for most of his stay. And that's why you wanted to know his full name and address?"

"Haha, yeah. Anyway, Helga and I would know when he came to visit her, so the next time he did, we'd send him another letter. It was, 'Hello once again, friend. Samba is sad. You see someone else. Samba good for you, Samba take good care of you, much better than that woman can. Give Samba chance to find out. Me much better for you.' Hah."

"She wondered why he stopped coming around but was very happy about it."

"Well, I didn't know you were like that, darling," said George.

"Alexander, I've been thinking about the Walers, mate. A friend of mine gave me a call to let me know that, if I needed anything sent to Australia, his steamer would be leaving in a week and to let him know. We could send them on a holiday, too, mate. If everything turns out well, I can bring them back. It's better to be safe, I suppose, mate."

"Of course. They're family, too. Give us the details and we'll fix that up straight away."

"Thanks, mate. I'll let him know."

Blue was glad to hit the sack after enjoyable talks around the fireplace, for it was the only time he could really think about the one big distraction in his life.

Seven

The general seeks support for his attempted coup

In December of 1916, Alexander received a letter from his good friend, a general in the Imperial Russian Army, requesting a visit to discuss important matters with him.

When the general arrived at the estate, he and Alexander spoke privately in the study after warming up around the fire. The general said, "I'll be frank with you, my friend, I'm drumming up support to overthrow that idiot."

"Heavens, Kroysie! Stage a coup? You can't be serious!"

"He's a fool! Can't you see that he's going to take us to hell with him the way he's going? The duma (parliament) is supporting us, now."

"Oh, yes, the puppets? But…"

"But what? It's not the right time? Or we could get killed? Or you think I might fail? Alexander, even his most loyal generals have considered taking drastic measures."

"Oh, no, so, things are that bad now, that it's come to this?"

"I'm afraid it's a matter of choosing sides, now, my good friend.

"We've got our own secret Intel gathering operation going, and it's been up and running for some time. We know who his most loyal are, Alexander. It's not just the generals who dislike the way he's handling the war effort. Trying to talk to him is like talking to a German who knows little Russian. And even that's got me thinking."

"You mean, Alexandria?"

"Yes, Alexandria, the German."

"Well, exactly how much support have you got?"

"We have enough generals and commissioned officers to do the job. I've also been discussing the possibility with certain members of the Central War Industries Committee. Everyone is on side unless a Tsarist plant or two are among them.

"Our Intel from the peasant sector paints an alarming picture, though. There's growing anarchy within the ranks of the Reserve Battalions in Petrograd. Out of the one hundred and eighty thousand troops there, you know, new recruits, experienced reservists from proletarian backgrounds, those from aristocracy, three thousand loyal police, about thirty thousand would be loyal to the fool. His loyal are greatly outnumbered.

"It's known that these troops with proletarian backgrounds, the ones who were forced to shoot their families in previous crowd-control confrontations, will be turning the tables next time. They've already decided that their officers will be shot if orders were issued to shoot their people.

"Alexander, that could happen very soon."

"What, on International Women's Day?"

"We haven't got Intel on that yet, but word is that women and girl students are planning another demonstration on that day. That'll happen, and you don't have to be a scientist to work it out. All workers and soldiers will sympathize with them."

"Oh, no, that doesn't sound too good at all, but you think you could stave off what seems to be the inevitable if you were to seize power?"

"I'm hoping that the people would be happy if I were to give them what they want before International Women's Day, and I could boost the morale of the troops by delegating to proper manage the war effort."

"That sounds good in theory, but just remember that Rasputin's involvement with Alexandra has made people furious, and tensions are hotting up…"

"I forgot to tell you. He was murdered."

"Rasputin?"

"Yes, at Moika Palace last night. I knew something was going to happen. They say it took quite a bit to kill him, too. He sure was a beast of a man."

"Who murdered him?"

"They say it was a group of conservative noblemen. Apparently, they say he was like a wild beast when he got shot."

"Yeah, I'm not surprised."

"What do you want me to do?"

"I'm basically wanting to know that you won't stab me in the back when it happens. I want to know where your loyalties lie."

"You know we think alike, and who knows, there just may be hope for us. I suppose anything is worth having a go if there's a slight glimmer of hope. You've got my support, friend. Just remember, even if you were to seize power, the people would still have a regime. Do they want that anymore?

"How bad are things in the queues, now?"

"I saw a queue of about eleven hundred people formed near a cooperative shop in Koslov. People waited ten days to buy flour that wasn't there."

Alexander shook his head and said, "The last time I read about it, people were queuing up at three o'clock in the morning in below-zero temperatures outside the Municipal Meat Markets. They were buying the scraps from the floor, for crying out loud."

"Alexander, I know I could work things out to feed

the people."

"Yes, I can only wish you luck, my friend, I certainly hope it works out for you."

"Yeah, 'God's speed' is the way to go, I'd rather depend on God than on luck. Sorry, I'm just so cranky, Alexander!"

"Aren't we all.

"Did you have any trouble with wolves on your way out here?"

"No."

"Have you got room for a passenger?"

"Yes, of course."

The governess went back to Petrograd with the general in his troika.

Days later, communications were disrupted when a blizzard engulfed the area. Thousands of trains carrying food and fuel to Petrograd were stranded, compounding an already dire situation.

The general's plans to attempt a coup gave a glimmer of hope to some members of the family, but they all knew deep down that it was not going to work. Labour control over production, the abolition of property rights, and the forming of a Soviet government were crucial features, the realisation of which, the people have been demanding for some time, but If the general were to give no consideration to their grievances in that area, they would see him as being just another tyrant. People knew that the abolition of property rights would be watered down to favour the landlords, anyway.

Grandpa was having second thoughts about staying in Russia. His decision would influence the rest of the Zuckschwerdt family, namely George's sister, Elizabeth, and her husband, Petrov, and their son, Alex. Everyone else, apart from those whose passage was already booked, had their own escape plans, which were discussed with all family members.

When Nikolai searched for personal papers in his wife's study to take to Australia with him, he came across a locked drawer in her desk and looked for a key in the other drawers. He found one that matched the lock, and when looking for what he was after, he noticed a huge bundle of letters bound together. He was curious to know what they were, and, without opening them, he looked at the back of each envelope for the return name and address.

He said to himself, "Addressed to Vera? What are they doing here? Capt. Bill Rawlings, London? Going back almost a year before she met George. All unopened, too? If she had no interest in him, she would've burnt them. I couldn't see her giving them to her mother.

"I'll go and ask Natasha what's going on."

He approached her in the family room and asked to speak with her in the kitchen.

Vera noticed them heading off and went to talk to them.

In the kitchen, Nikolai said, "I found these in your

desk drawer. You have obviously kept them from her, but I want to know why? You know she was devastated thinking that he left her. Just tell me why!"

Vera stopped at the kitchen door to take her slipper off to clear some grit, but she got there in time to hear the question her father asked. She put her slipper on and studied the letters in her father's hand as she stood at the doorway in shock.

"What are you doing going through my personal stuff?" asserted Natasha.

"Well, this looks like Vera's personal stuff to me. What's going on?"

"Look, that soldier has no title. Besides, he wants to take her to London to live, and she's adored by a handsome prince."

"I can't believe what I'm hearing!"

Vera's heart sank, and her jaw dropped as she stood and watched in disbelief.

Mixed emotions engulfed her as rage was taking hold.

George came up to her, and when he saw the look of horror on her face, he turned and listened to her mother finish what she was saying.

"George isn't exactly a prince, but he's got a title, unlike that common soldier."

"How could you do this to me! You are supposed to love me, not destroy me! I want my letters, now! If you don't mind!" she asserted, crying as she hurried to her.

They stood in shock when realising they were caught out.

Nikolai was so stunned that he could only blink when she snatched the letters out of his hand and ran out.

George's focus was on the bundle of letters when Vera ran past him.

Her mother stood watching her run off showing no regret or remorse.

He hurried to catch up with her, and when she got to her room, she slammed the door behind her. When George reached her door, he cried out to speak with her.

"Not now, George!"

He thought for a while and went back to see Nikolai. He said, "What's with the letters?"

"I think you better ask her mother, George."

"I suppose I'll have to explain myself, now. Come and sit in the family room.

"A year before she met you, she fell head over heels in love with an army officer from England. I couldn't let the relationship continue. It would've been an embarrassment for the family…"

"Now that you put your foot in your mouth, just make sure you don't put the other one in too," said Nikolai.

She looked at him in astonishment as he left the room.

George looked at her for a short while in astonishment and said nothing. He walked from the room deep in thought with his head down.

"Darling, I'm sorry," said Nikolai, knocking quietly on Vera's door upon hearing her sobbing.

"It's okay, Dad."

George stopped to look down the hallway, wondering if he should leave her alone. He went straight to his room and lay on his bed thinking for hours. He thought, "That'd destroy me too." His heart sank. He knew that he may very well have to condition his acceptance of a bleak outcome.

"Is Vera alright, Nikolai? I heard her crying." Alexander was informed when they went to the study.

The next morning, George knocked on her door. "I bought you some breakfast, darling."

"Come in, George."

"Oh, look, I just want to see you happy. If getting back with him is going to do that, do it. I had a good think about it, and I don't want you being miserable for the rest of your life."

"Oh, George, I thought he left me."

"I know, you told me a few times. I helped you get over it, didn't I?"

"Ahhhhhhhhhh, mother! How could she do this to me?"

"Well, that's aristocracy. That's why we're together."

"In his last letter, he told me that every time he rang…"

"What, here?"

"No, mum's place before I met you. Mother told him that I don't want him anymore."

He shook his head and said, "I'm not surprised."

"This letter is only recent. He wants me to tell him we're through, and he'll be in Petrograd on the 29th of February. He's been sent to the front and doesn't know how long mail takes to reach home."

"Well, I hope you get a letter before we go."

"Yeah, there's no way I can contact him."

In December, the Orloff family left for Australia, and they were happy to go, too.

The estate was receiving above-average snowfall at the start of the New Year.

The family persuaded Grandpa to go to Australia with them, as the general's hopes to secure power only reached the grounds of Winter Palace.

Personal trunks were packed, and there was much debate in which it was decided by senior family members to leave behind bulky heirlooms. Nikolai and his family took a lot of the most precious gemstones and heirlooms with them to Australia just in case. It would be impractical to flee from insurgents with truckloads of bulky furniture to deal with. Besides, that would be telling them exactly who you were.

Two days before their ship's expected time of departure from Petrograd, the trunks were loaded into two snowplough lorries. Arrangements were made for

Alexander's ex-serf friends to occupy the estate with other Zuckschwerdt family members, those who were staying, to take care of the livestock and to maintain the place until their return.

Many happy memories of life at the estate were shared, and Blue was captivated by the romance and intrigue of it all. He sincerely hoped that things would improve so that once again they could continue life there. It was home.

Blue could not sleep much, as he was still wrestling with those old mates of his, the ones who wore the Jersey of the preconceived old-fashioned ideas and attitudes. He kept asking himself, "How can it be, mate! Why can't I marry her? If she wants to marry me when she's an adult, there's nothing anyone can do about it. It's her choice."

He wrestled for hours with every issue concerning a relationship with her.

Monica could not sleep at all, as she was struggling to work out why he was reluctant to commit to a relationship. The words he uttered had been mulled over by her for all the possibilities. She thought, "He won't commit to me because I'm underage. I know it is."

Eight

Blue and the nobles drive straight into the revolution of Feb. 26, 1917

Early in the morning of Sunday, February 26,1917, (Julian calendar) three days after International Women Day, the lorries were crank started in the barn and warmed up. The women and girls were divided up and seated around the luggage in the back of the two canvas-covered snowplough lorries.

Alexander drove the lead lorry with Blue as his passenger while George drove the other lorry with Grandpa.

Frequent traffic on the road by those involved in demonstrations in Petrograd had already turned the snow and ice into slush, but the plough on the lorries made easy work of clearing the bulk of it away to enable good traction.

Because of the high risk of getting bogged while driving, Alexander planted his foot on the accelerator to get some speed up and alerted the girls to brace for a rough ride.

The deep ruts acted like tram tracks with sharp turns, and the only thing that could get them into trouble was having to stop for some reason.

"This is good, Blue."

"Yeah, mate. Hope it stays this way."

"Heavens! Is that a moose on the road up ahead?"

"I reckon it is, mate. He's injured, too!"

"Ah, the klaxon's (horn) broken, but I'm not stopping. Brace yourselves in the back!"

The huge bull was limping ever so slowly toward the edge of the road, so Blue drew his revolver and fired off one shot in the air outside the window attempting to hurry it along.

Alexander knew that he should stay in the ruts of the road and not try to go around the beast, for he could quite easily lose control of the lorry if he were to do so.

The girls screamed as one side of the plough slammed into the beast's backside with a loud impact. George's suspicions were confirmed when he saw the large animal slam into a tree off the road, as his vision was blocked by the truck in front and could not see the beast. The impact was so great that the tree split, shaking every bit of snow from its branches.

"Ah! I hope there's no damage," said Alexander.

"Does the steering feel alright, mate?"

"Yeah, everything feels okay."

"I'll know if there's something wrong, mate." They bounced around on the bench seat that was designed for everything but comfort.

"Oh, that feels better. The road is much better to drive on now," said Alexander.

After a couple of hours of sliding around on the slushy road, Petrograd was in sight.

Before long, they were approaching the congestion on the way to Kazan Cathedral.

Alexander said, "Everyone in the city must be out today." They stopped to witness demonstrators menacingly surging on police lines outside a government building.

A tram was being overturned by a mob. People were running and screaming toward a car which had soldiers with rifles lying on its wheel guards and standing on the side steps hanging on to the roof. When the car sped off, one soldier lost his rifle while trying to hold on.

"Oh, mate! There must be thousands of police here, all in combat gear, too."

"The governor would have the full complement out in force, both the Special Corps of Gendarmes, and the Reserve Battalions. And look at the troublemakers.

"God help us! It looks like they'll keep going until they get what they want. If I know Nicholas, he'd have ignored the first wire he should've got from the governor by now. Alexandria has somehow convinced him that the fat man is a nuisance, and it's had a big influence on his views of the governor.

"I bet that he's already wired back a message reading, 'Don't bother me with matters of little consequence!' as he always does when confronted with a challenge. I wonder if the governor has already sent the message, 'Overthrow is imminent?' He'll give orders to deplete the crowd with rifle fire. It doesn't look good. Revolution is imminent.

"It'd be just like the last revolution in 1905, Blue, only this time he won't be tolerated. Since then, he's broken all his promises with force. People just don't trust him anymore."

Alexander and Blue met up with those from the other lorry as they walked to the back of it to watch the demonstrators, many of whom frightened the girls as they ran past screaming and surging on police lines with all sorts of objects that were used as weapons.

"Sis, I'm scared!" cried Natty as she put her arms around Vera's waist.

Vera put her hand on Natty's back and said, "I know, we all are. Just know that everything's going to be fine. You know that my prayers are always answered."

"Okay, sis."

The clash was violent, and the police on horseback were excessive with their punishment on the crowd. No one was exempt from the brutality, not even the children. Blood stained many faces, and many people were being helped away but some lay injured on the street without assistance from anyone.

As they watched the heated clash unfold, which spooked some of the police horses and made them rear, several mounted Cossacks moved in from behind the weakened police cordon. Their sights firmly set on the individual in police combat gear yelling orders to shoot the demonstrators.

When the other policemen saw the Cossacks move in, they were reluctant to use their weapons. But the police officer giving orders countermanded the orders yelled out to police from the highest-ranking Cossack to holster their weapons. The police officer screamed, "I only take orders from the Tsar, you have the same orders, too!

"Shoot that man causing trouble! Shoot!"

When the police officer giving orders was about to shoot a man for whacking his horse, making it rear, the Cossack drew his service revolver and shot him once in the head. The policeman crashed to the ground from his mount where he was trampled on by his distressed horse as it bolted.

Natty cried out loud when she witnessed the terrible event and looked away as Vera covered her terrified sister's face with her hands. Monica and young Alex stood in disbelief, and Vera shook her head, as the incident reminded her of past atrocities inflicted on the people by the regime.

One policeman was pulled from his mount by demonstrators close by as he drew his weapon to fire upon the head Cossack. Other policemen looked at one another, then looked over at the Cossacks with their hands on their holstered service revolvers as more Cossacks rode up behind them.

With weapons trained on them by the Cossacks, the police were then apprehended and quickly disarmed before being escorted from the cordon.

People ran in all directions when more shots rang out close by, but they were unaware that the Cossacks were rounding up police. Those who stayed, knew that rifle fire was directed at the police who resisted and not at the demonstrators, and their mood quickly changed as they realised that they had the support that they thought they would never get.

Their anger and motivation to fight was put on hold while they cheered and chanted their support for the young Cossack recruits who took control of the cordon. And women and girls reached out to hold their hands. The Cossacks showed their allegiance to the proletariat by reaching out and holding theirs while the police were being escorted away. Their weapons were collected and distributed to the men in the crowd, and they were eager to receive them.

The police knew that they were outnumbered considerably by the soldiers from the Reserve Battalions, and they also knew that they would have to either die for the Tsar or surrender, the former was considered a fool's option, despite their loyalty to the Romanovs. The other option was to just join the other side, as to surrender, one would have to be guilty of a war crime.

Alexander knew that the incident was the beginning of the end, and he needed to retrieve important documentation from the mansion. He decided to go to the textile factory to use the company car to do what he had to do, and Blue could drive the lorry after some basic instructions on the handling of the capricious truck that had a mind of its own.

As Alexander drove into one of the less congested backstreets not far from his factory, he saw a mob outside a factory looking up and pointing in their direction while arming themselves with what appeared to be pipes, tools, and all sorts of weapon-like objects. As more people emerged from the factory, the mob started running toward the two lorries.

"Oh, what does that look like to you, Blue?"

"Well, my intuition tells me that something is about to erupt, but I don't think they're after us."

"Blue, could you get out and tell George to drive into that street behind us and take the back roads to the factory. Tell him to hurry up, too!

"Get ready to hang on, girls!"

The street was too narrow for the lorry to negotiate

a turn, as Alexander stopped just past the street that George was told to turn into. He waited for George to turn into the street while constantly checking on the workers.

The mob may not have been chasing after them, but Alexander was prepared to be embarrassed rather than put his family at risk by waiting around to find out.

"You're right to go now, mate, he's gone. Hang on in the back!"

The lorry's crash gearbox was grinding when Alexander was forcing the gear lever at revs that were higher than normal to engage reverse gear with the clutch depressed. This would normally have been done at low revs having reduced grind on the gearbox, but it would increase the potential for the engine to stall, especially with a heavy load. It was something that he wanted to avoid, as the mob would surely have reached them by the time the crank handle was turned to start the engine again, should that be the case.

When he engaged reverse gear, he revved the engine before he dropped (released) the clutch for fear of stalling the truck. The lorry was motionless, and there was an almighty bang, after which, a loud clunking noise followed and continued until the engine stopped.

Blue looked at Alexander and said nothing, but they both knew that the diff had just expired in a dramatic way.

The mob reached the lorry, and Alexander leaned

back towards Blue praying hard to himself as a stocky worker ran to the driver's window with a meat cleaver. Others moved in around the door, and they soon surrounded the entire vehicle.

Blue had his hand on his revolver as the man said, "We heard shooting, have you seen or heard anything?"

A relieved Alexander said, "Oh, yeah! Cossacks were shooting at police who were dishing it out to demonstrators."

"Spasibo," said the man before he and his co-workers ran off in the direction whence the lorries came.

The pair looked at each other, and Blue smiled as he shook his head. Alexander then shook his head and said, "I'm too old for this! They're not going to put up with any lies this time, Blue. I'm afraid there's going to be a lot of bloodshed, too."

George stopped a short distance down the street to wait for Alexander, and when the lorry appeared to be in trouble, he got out of his lorry and stood on the road next to the driver's door. He observed with his revolver in hand in case there was trouble. When he saw that the men had gone without incident, he holstered his revolver and got in the lorry to reverse back to the others.

"Thanks for waiting, George. Could you and Blue go to the factory and bring back one of the lorries from there, please?"

The girls and Grandpa waited by the roadside discussing the chain of events that transpired. The brave face that each of them expected masked their apprehension until their tears revealed the truth.

The factory manager drove the company car back to greet Alexander. Lukas said, "The lines were down, and I couldn't reach you because the switch board was jammed when they were repaired."

"Not a problem, Lukas. Everyone okay?"

"Women from the other textile factories came around to drum up support to demonstrate in the city centre. They were absent on International Women's Day because they went to a Bolshevik cram session and went to Nevsky Prospekt (main street in city centre) with their placards. They talked a lot of the men into joining them, too.

"Thousands of people were forced back from the blockade on the bridge yesterday, so they crossed the river on unstable ice. Four people were killed at Nevsky Prospekt yesterday, too. It's getting worse. The last of the workers left a while ago to join the mob.

"There's no trams, no taxi's, or anything else operating, anywhere. It's utter chaos, and just about the whole city is out on the streets demonstrating. They want change."

"Yeah, okay, Lukas, I better get going before the mansions are sacked. They most likely have been already."

"Oh, Elizabeth said they left the mansion and will be at your brother's place."

"Thank you. Lock up when George gets the lorry.

"Wait for me there when you've finished loading the lorry. Come and find me if I'm not home by then.

"George, give me a gun! Better give me ammo, too."

He made his way to the mansion.

"Pray for him, Vera." George shook his head.

At Vladimir's place, they were greeted by the family and discussed the alarming change of atmosphere that was obviously getting out of hand. Apprehension worried everyone sick, and it was starting to show when some of them were forgetting things.

Vladimir and his lot decided to pack up and leave, too.

At six o'clock, George took Vladimir's prestige motor car to try to find Alexander.

"The car might not be the same when I bring it back, uncle."

"Don't worry about it, just go and find the old fool and bring him back."

The pair took extra ammo and drove the long way to the mansion to avoid hostilities in and around the city centre where sporadic gunfire was heard.

In the twilight, they stopped when they approached a dense angry mob. Seconds later, they heard gunfire ringing out. They were alarmed when they saw thousands of people running in all directions trying to avoid injury or death.

Demonstrators followed soldiers on an attack on

police, they knew that they had the support they needed, so they were motivated to attack.

The mob overturned police vehicles, setting them alight as police fled. They cheered the mounted Cossacks and kept up with them. When gunfire was heard, some Cossacks made haste to a bridge where a barricade was being erected by police to prevent more demonstrators amassing on the city centre.

George decided to detour, taking the long way to the mansion. Shortly after, they were faced with a mob running towards them out of the thick black toxic smoke that filled the cold night air.

The passenger's side of the split windshield suddenly shattered, spraying glass over Blue as gunshots were heard. "Are you okay, Blue?"

"Yeah, mate." He bent over and shook his head to remove the glass.

"Hang on, I'm getting us out of here!" He turned the steering wheel suddenly and put his foot hard on the accelerator.

"Oh, beauty, mate, you know how to handle this thing!" He fishtailed it and sprayed mud and slush over the mob in their wake. "I think we would've been better off taking the jalopy, mate. This thing draws too much attention."

"You're right."

They finally reached the mansion where looters were running from its manicured gardens with their stash.

"Well, there's no jalopy! Here, mate." He threw a box of ammo.

Both men entered the building and, when inside, they went in different directions to search the rooms upstairs.

As George was about to enter the first room, he was bailed over by a man whose vision was obstructed by the large item of furniture he was carrying out of a bedroom in a hurry. The man screamed, "Don't shoot!" as he had a gun pointed at him.

The man saw no one fitting Alexander's description when asked of him, and after a thorough search of the building, George discovered that the safe in Alexander's room had been opened and left unlocked.

"We'll take the short route home and come back the long one. He must be on one."

The smoke from many government buildings, that burned unattended, was choking them as they waited at an intersection of a congested street. The police cordon was breaking as hundreds of demonstrators pushed several heavy-laden vehicles toward it after setting them alight. Other unladen lorries and cars were used to transport the wounded and cart the dead. The situation worsened when dense toxic smoke from one of the burning lorries choked everyone. "Oh, mate, they must be burning rubber!" They decided to detour and come back onto the route further down the road.

Vladimir and Fiona drove to the hospital hoping for

a miracle, but they knew everyone would be too busy there. When they got there, they offered their assistance, hoping to come across him.

When George got back to the house, he asked Blue to stay with Vera and the girls in case Alexander showed up while he took off to the hospital to help.

The girls were crying and holding onto Vera.

At the hospital, George had to park three streets away. The immediate area around its car park was congested with private vehicles, and there was a tabletop lorry from which men were removing bodies outside the adjoining mortuary.

The incoming wounded were quickly occupying the car park as they were left on their stretchers awaiting doctors to examine them for priority tagging. Some seasoned nurses expressed their horror at the worst of the wounds as they each held a lantern to them.

"If you're not here to help, young man, leave immediately!" shouted a doctor who clearly was in no mood to suffer fools or sightseers lightly.

"I'm here to help, so give me a job!" He knew that he was unable to carry out a search any other way.

"Go inside and tell someone that doctor Popimple sent you to help. They'll soon give you a job."

George tried to get a visual on as many faces as he possibly could. He knew it would take a couple of weeks to find his father in that environment, but he had to give the search a chance.

He started to wonder if it would be best if he were to concentrate his efforts on the streets again, but he decided that he would stay for a few hours before doing that. Early that night, he left the hospital knowing that other family members were persisting there.

While George was driving back to the house, he caught up with a car that slowly became visible out of the dense smog which engulfed most of the city. After a while he heard gunshots ringing out close by. The driver of the car in front swerved violently and lost control when someone ran out in front of it. The driver was thrown out when his car careered off the road and rolled several times.

George stopped to help, but there was little he could do for the man whose brains were steaming in the cold night air as they spewed from his crushed skull in the snow.

George thought, "He'd probably still be alive if he didn't swerve." He shook his head.

As he was protected from the tragic side of life in his upbringing, he was sickened by the incident, and he felt too sick to drive anymore that night. He screamed, "Where the heck are you, Dad? You can't leave me now!"

When George arrived back at the house, he was discussing options with family who had come back from the hospital. A knock on the front door changed the bleak mood to hope.

"Dad! Where have you been?" Everyone rushed to

greet him.

"I got bashed at the mansion! Someone dragged me out of the car and punched me in the face because he wanted my car. He drove off, and I started walking, still in shock.

"I got caught up in a shootout and almost got run over a couple of times. I had to lay low and dodge bullets. A couple of hours of that and I was on my way, but I needed to rest somewhere, so I sat on a park bench and just collapsed on it.

"Some kindly person woke me and asked if I was okay, so I found the strength to keep going, and here I am."

"We were so worried about you. We've got to get out of this place!" said Elizabeth.

"Oh, no! What'll it be like at the harbour?" queried George.

"Chaos, I imagine," said Elizabeth.

"Heavens, I don't know if the ship will still be there. Will we go tomorrow?"

"Why can't we go tonight?" asked Adelaide.

"I don't think there'll be anyone there. The mob's probably going after the navy ships. If the place is still operational, there might be a couple of workers there tomorrow. At least we'll be able to see what's going on, anyway," said Alexander.

"Yeah, tomorrow it is, then," said Elizabeth.

"I've got to pick up Esther," said Fiona.

"Her sister wants to come, too," said Vladimir.

"Heavens, there's only four hours to sunup. You better get going right now. How long will you be?"

"I don't know, but we'll go to the harbour from there. If we're not there by sunup, we most probably will have run into trouble and put in place our alternative plan to egress. I love you, my brother."

Alexander thought of those words as Vladimir and his lot drove off.

Nine

The noble family's escape from hostilities in Petrograd on their friend's steamer

The German government had recently resumed its unrestricted submarine warfare offensive after a period of passivity. The previous back off was consequential to the outrage pressure from the United States of America and other neutral countries for the sinking of the passenger ship Lusitania in 1915. Eleven hundred and ninety-eight innocent people lost their lives as a result.

Germany was unwilling to provoke America into entering the war, and she also knew that her assertions that Great Britain's blockades were both illegal and immoral, in their eyes, would only fall on deaf ears in America.

The British naval blockades were having their desired effect on Germany's capability to survive. She was desperate, so she was motivated to build a bigger and better fleet of killer long-range U-boats for commerce raiding. It was a do-or-die situation where all ships suspected of carrying contraband to the British Isles were sunk.

The German government argued that a sub's crew was unable to do what was required of them by the Allies to meet conditions set out in the Prize Law Regulations, that is to board ships, inspect the shipment, and ensure ship's crew safety and more. Anyway, it would bog them down with policing activities where time would be lost searching compliant ships while other ones carrying contraband would slip past.

With the increased threat from beneath the surface, the British were actively engaged in pursuing counter-measures, especially in detection and underwater bombs.

Utilizing art for military purposes was being exploited worldwide. The French used it to disguise their airfields to avoid or escape bombing raids, likening them to farm buildings and orchards when viewed from the air. The navy used cubism art on their ships to create optical illusions when under threat from German U-boat attacks.

Because the Prize Law Regulations were being ignored by the Germans, where proper action, in the eyes of the world, wasn't taken by their ships of war that operated against merchant shipping, Great Britain was trying to keep secret her 'Q-ship' operations, which was a merchant ship with concealed weapons.

It was designed to lure a U-boat to the surface. The sub's crew would then man the forward deck gun to fire a high explosive round at the waterline of the ship's beam to sink it. That being a cheaper option, rather than using expensive torpedoes, five of which would be carried when on a mission. Torpedos would normally be saved for the heavy-laden ships that carried munitions and heavy equipment.

The Q-ship would then hoist the white ensign and fire several rounds off when its concealed gun was brought to bear. By the time the U-boat skipper realised that it was a trap, the conning tower would be blasted from the sub.

One clever passenger ship captain had the notion to use the camouflage concept on his ship when a friend of his in high command in England confided in him as to its potential.

Because camouflage was associated with the military, he would not only arouse the enemy's suspicion, but he would also cause confusion when in the sights of an enemy periscope. He would pursue all avenues necessary for survival, so he put artists to work on his ship in the hope that some U-boat skippers may have been aware of the trap. He was thinking it would be common knowledge soon, and then the enemy would be reluctant to attack his ship if they thought it were a trap.

The camouflaged passenger ship was in the harbour where its crew was sorting supplies while the skipper was at the port authority head office.

Officers on Russian navy ships close by who were known to be loyal to the Tsar were being shot, and the commandeering of the Baltic fleet was in progress.

A day after they were booked for passage, Alexander and his lot knew that they would be stranded in the harbour. They went to the passenger terminal, anyway, despite the danger and uncertainty amid the chaos.

Somehow, through all the confusion, the harbour authority was still operating, despite the challenge of having a skeleton crew. The absence of some highly skilled maritime workers who took off to join the demonstrators or flee the insurgents was a problem that faced the ships' captains, but they were resolved by the utilization of specialist crew members.

When they reached the ship that they had booked passage on, they saw that its deck was being crammed with military personnel who were also fleeing. Standing room only was the order of the day.

"Heavens above, what's this all about?" Alexander shouted at its captain from the dock.

"Get aboard, if you want to!" screamed the captain.

"Is that you, Alexander?"

"Alexei, what are you doing here?"

"I just docked yesterday. Looking for someone

to operate the water pump for me. It looks like I help myself again.

"Good move, getting out of this place. You must've dodged a few bullets, too, hey?"

"Oh, you don't know the half of it."

"I've heard that, a committee of the duma is appointing a provisional government. A 'Dual Power' to succeed the autocracy. Apparently, the workers and soldiers have only just formed the Petrograd Soviet of Workers' and Soldiers' Deputies that form the other part," said Alexei.

"Oh, yes, they're the so-called 'Radical Intellectuals' who claim to represent the socialist parties. You must look out for them, and they'll be an official power soon, looking forward to giving their very first order in a couple of days. You know what that'll be, don't you?"

"Yeah, what the Romanovs and all of aristocracy fear most, that the 'military take orders from it only' and not from the provisional government. Now you know why I want to pull out straight away, or as soon as I can. But it looks like they're in power already."

A few gunshots were heard coming from one of the navy ships close by.

"See what I mean. A lot of military and government bigwigs have begged me to get them out of here, Alexander.

"I've accrued a small fortune but forget about overcrowding like this one. He sounds like a pirate. Some people are so desperate that they trade gold bullion for fishing boats, offering sixfold the cost of the boat in some cases."

"Goodness. Sorry, this is Blue, and you know the rest of us."

"G'day, mate. How are you?"

"Oh, an Australian! How refreshing. Pleased to meet you."

"Likewise, mate."

Elizabeth said, "Vladimir and the rest haven't turned up yet. Where could they be? I'm so worried about them."

Alexander said, "We're all worried. All we can do is wait here for as long as possible.

"Alexei is another retired commander, Blue, we served together in the Russo-Japanese War.

"Where are you headed, anyway, Alexei?"

"Australia."

"Yeah! That's where we're going, but my brother and his family haven't turned up."

"Oh, I…"

"Heaven! What's that?" he shouted when shots rang out on a navy ship.

"We better get going. Come with me, but I must go very soon, my ship might be next, and this is the only opportunity that we all have. We'll have to leave as soon as I fill the tanks."

"There's someone. Excuse me, can you sort out my paperwork, please?" asked Alexander.

"I was about to go. Hurry up, then." The man appeared to be anxious to join his fellow workers, but he took the family to the counter where he sorted the paperwork.

Alexi summoned help from his crew to fill the water tanks, and when the job was done, he met up with Blue and the family as they were coming out of the terminal.

"Is everyone right to go?"

"Thank God, yes," said Alexander as he scanned the terminal for any sign of Vladimir.

"They look like trouble, mate." A motor car jam-packed with soldiers stopped nearby. Men with rifles slid off the wheel guards, jumped off the side boards, and clambered out through the doors.

A man who was giving orders to his men looked in the direction of the family and started walking over.

"Pretend you're not good at speaking Russian, mate."

"I wondered why you were dressed like that," said Alexei. "Good disguise."

When the man approached the family, he said in Russian, "Are you all leaving?" as he was looking at Alexander.

"G'day, mate, I take it you're in charge?" He handed the man his papers, hoping that it would bring the man's attention to himself and away from Alexander.

"Australian? Why are you leaving?"

"We were hoping to do some business, but the regime has been stuffing us around something shocking."

"What kind of business?"

"Waler horses."

"Oh, Yes, I've seen them in action, and I've heard a lot about your countrymen. Australians with Walers in war are a formidable force. I assure you that you'll not be, as you say it, 'stuffed around' again, if you decide to come back. In fact, I hope you will come back to do business with us, soon, that is."

The man was checking the luggage carefully, but his focus of attention was on Alexander. In English, the man said, "I have to check your bags?"

Alexander said nothing because he knew he sounded like a Russian when he spoke English, he just made a gesture with his hand and nodded his head for yes. He did well not to show concern about carrying Russian paperwork.

When the man was checking the bags, everyone could see that he was squeezing the hems and carefully studying bulky items.

The man spoke to Alexander in Russian. "Ummmmmm," uttered Alexander as he turned to Blue who knew the language enough to understand what he said, thankfully.

"He said, 'What's that sticking out of your coat?' That's all." Alexander looked down at his coat and then at the man.

Blue knew he would have to do something before the man cottoned on to the fact that the group was anything but what it appeared to be, so he tried to think of a distraction. He had to think of something quick, as the man handed Blue his papers and was about to ask Alexander for his as his hand went straight from Blue to him.

Alexei could see that his friend was in a bit of a spot, so he made a move and said, "Excuse me, sir."

"Who are you?"

"I'm the captain of the ship they've got passage on…"

One of the man's subordinates screamed, "Sir, the passengers on that ship are trying to hide."

The man in charge turned to see what ship his man was pointing to and screamed, "Make sure the ship doesn't leave port!"

"How do I do that, sir?" screamed his subordinate.

"Ask him if he wouldn't mind sticking around for a while!" he screamed. "What do you think?" He shook his head. "Shoot anyone who touches those mooring lines and wait for me! Call the rest of the men!" he screamed then turned to Alexei and pointed. "Is that your ship?"

"Mine's further down. Sir, if you don't mind, I've got to get these Australians onboard."

"When I'm ready!" The man brought his attention back to Alexander.

"Hello, you're handsome! You can check me out any time you like but take your time. I'd like to come back for another holiday, that is, if you're around," said Monica who spoke fluent English and mimicked Blue's slang to a tee.

When his eyes turned to Monica, she gave him a big smile. He said, "Who are you?"

"I'm his daughter, Monica," She pointing to Blue and kept smiling.

Blue's eyes said it all.

"Emmmm, aharrrrr. May I check your bag, then?"

"Yeah, sure, mate. You can check me out, too."

Blue's eyes opened wider.

"Ummm, no need to. Thank you for being so cooperative…"

One of the insurgents screamed, "Sir, they're getting away!"

"Stay here," said the man as he ran to a ship nearby.

"Let's get the hell out of here!" said Alexei in a low tone of voice.

As they were starting to make some ground toward Alexie's ship, the man screamed, "Stop!"

The group stopped and waited for the man to run back.

"I haven't finished with you."

Alexei pulled the last one out of his hat and said, "That ship over there has got lots of Russian officers onboard," and pointing to the one Alexander booked passage on.

The man turned to see the ship and called out to his men who were nowhere to be seen.

The man ran back to find his men.

"Let's get the hell out of here!" asserted Alexei with a low voice.

They hurried to his ship and breathed a sigh of relief when onboard. Alexei said, "Demetri, get us out of here! Right now! Please."

"What about the pilot?"

"You know your way out of here. Just get going! Don't worry about rules and regulations, now!"

"You're trembling, skipper. Are you okay?"

"I'm okay. I just had a vision of my worst nightmare happening to us. You should see Alexander. He's a gibbering idiot. He was going at the knees on the way to the ship. I had to help him along."

"Shit! You're right, Alexei."

"Dad, you're rattling!"

"Release mooring lines, fore and aft!" shouted Demetri. "I'll take her out of port, skipper.

"That Russian down there is waving both arms at us, skipper."

"Everyone, wave back and smile!" said Alexi in a low voice.

"Oh! Where do you keep the Vodka?" groaned Alexander.

"Good idea. Come to my cabin, friends. You're still a bit wonky, Alexander."

"Merciful heavens! I was fearless in my younger days, but now..." He shook his head.

Although deeply saddened that other family

members missed departure, they were greatly relieved when they were well and truly into the Baltic. "Merciful God, I hope nothing's happened to them. I hope they're alright."

There was silence for a while, and everyone was trying to settle their nerves. They just collapsed in one of their cabins with Alexei who got the Vodka out.

After a while, Blue said, "What's the fancy paint work for, mate?"

"Hopefully, to make U-boat skippers think twice before they attack my ship. It's pretty risky business operating a steamer nowadays."

"Oh, yeah, Q-ship?" said Alexander.

"I see you've been informed, too," said Alexei.

"You do know that some of my best friends are generals, too?

"I'm feeling a lot better, now, thank goodness."

"Oh, good, I was worried about you," said Alexei.

"Yes, Blue, the 'dazzle decorated' concept, works for me I feel. Too bad you missed seeing the sides. I commissioned the artists to paint the stern to make it look like the bow when viewed longitudinally and to paint the bow to make it look like the stern when viewed the same way, and I got them to paint a few stripes amidships too.

"If my ship, traveling with the actual wind, were to be viewed through a periscope longitudinally, the smoke from the stack would be blown fore. Are you with me?"

"Of course, it'd look like it's traveling in a direction that's counter to its true course," said Alexander.

"I forgot to get the artists to do the smokestack. Looks funny with the stack leaning the same way the ship's going. I might get my men to do it.

"And, Alexander, the dazzle effect alone would distort the visual firing control systems. It'd be extremely hard for a sub's skipper to gauge the size, the speed, the course, and the range of the ship. They'd have a lot of trouble trying to fix a proper bearing on it for a torpedo attack. If they were to let one loose, the skipper's calculations could be out as much as fifty-six degrees, missing the ship entirely."

"Yeah, the skipper would then be left with the unpleasant stigma affecting the morale of his crew, not to mention the loss of an expensive torpedo," said Alexander.

"When a crew starts doubting the competency of their skipper, they may as well stick him in a tube to let him loose like a torpedo," said Alexei.

On the first night of the voyage, Alexei enforced a strict lights curfew. U-boats travelled on the surface to save fuel on dark nights. Lookouts on both ship and sub would have their binoculars out searching for any sign of light.

During the day, Alexei would resume a zigzag course and vary the speed on different legs of it as a precautionary measure, making it a lot harder for a U-boat skipper to gain a proper bearing on his ship.

He made the family feel comfortable in their cabins, and those who were interested were invited to spend time on the bridge with him during the day. He specifically requested the company of the men, all of whom had military backgrounds. Four good brains were better than one when faced with a situation with the enemy.

They were in submarine waters in the Baltic Sea. And if they were to survive that, they then had to brave the waters in the warzone surrounding the British Isles, which was without a doubt the worst to come.

It was a bit uncomfortable having to squeeze six people into a small cabin, but there were no complaints.

The women and the girls were showing signs of anxiety. They stayed together and rested while supporting each other with thought-provoking activities.

Everyone was tired and needed sleep. Alexei, however, somehow survived on little or none but was something he changed. He needed to be alert.

Blue got to bed but had no sleep. He was still confused about Monica, but he eventually dozed off.

Monica got to bed and stayed awake for hours thinking about his words. She thought, "I wonder if he's thinking of me? When I fell on him having that pillow fight, he was reluctant to move. Emmmm, and in the barn, too, surely, he's interested in me?"

Ten

A German sub threat to sink the steamer is challenged

The next day, moderate sea state conditions with light winds provided a good change, especially when one's bones suffered from constant pounding by chilly winds in the top castles of the crow's nests, usually in foul weather.

The welfare of the passengers and crew was dependent upon the skills and the keen eyes behind the binoculars of the lookouts who never complained, and Alexei responded to their calls with the utmost urgency.

"Good morning, did you have a good night's sleep?" Alexei greeted Alexander, Grandpa, George, and Blue on the bridge.

Everyone responded with a 'yes' except Blue who looked a bit seasick. He just looked at Alexei. "Coffee, anyone?"

"Oh, beauty, mate. I haven't had one in ages."

"I'd prefer foul weather.

"Any updates on U-boat activity? Anyone got any ideas on how to deal with them?"

"Nah, mate. But I've heard about a ship ramming a sub's conning tower."

Alexei said, "Ah, huh, me too. Heard a few stories, all straight from the horse's mouth. One skipper said, 'In hindsight, I could quite easily have rammed the sub that sunk my ship before its crew could even fire off one round from the deck guns.'

"He's been punishing himself ever since for not taking the initiative to do so. The captain I spoke to wasn't experienced. He lacked perception and native wit.

"One captain said he had a perfect opportunity to ram a sub when it surfaced on his starboard beam. In the time that it took its crew to get out and put the breach in the forward deck gun, then load and traverse the gun for a waterline shot, he could quite easily have powered towards it and rammed it. There was nothing he could've done but dive with his crew on deck. And they would've had trouble trying to get the breach out of the gun when realising they were the ones under attack. They would've had to jump overboard, had the ship's captain decided to go for a ram. And even then, the ship would've hit the conning tower, anyway.

"The sub's skipper could've ordered his crew to start shooting, but at what? If you blast away at the bow, the ship's going to keep coming, isn't it? No way would it sink before it got to the sub. And under full steam, too. What would you do? Panic of course."

Grandpa said, "Wouldn't you think it'd be a normal reaction to ram it, anyway? Just sitting there watching someone prepare to kill you and doing nothing about it sounds stupid to me."

Alexei said, "It's a survival thing, isn't it? It all boils down to 'who's behind the helm' on the day."

"Periscope off the Port beam!" screamed the lookout on the main crow's nest.

"Where? Where is he?" Alexei yelled as he went for his binoculars.

"There, skipper." Demetri pointed. "It's alright, he hasn't taken up a position to fix a bearing on us. On a parallel course with us. He thought he'd hit us with a shell instead of wasting a torpedo."

"Heavens give us steam!"

"Oh, yes, I see him! Lifeboat teams, standby with hammers (to release snubbing chain pins to lower lifeboats) on both port and starboard!" he ordered. "That's a relief. That gives us a bit of time to think.

"We were only just talking about this. Well, I think we know what to do, now.

"Half ahead, Demetri."

"Aye, skipper." He pulled the handle up on the E.O.T.

(engine order telegraph, from bridge to engine room) to slow speed.

Alexei said, "I'm hoping to better position the ship to attempt a ram on the conning tower, should he surface. He'll be history if he chooses that for his plan of action.

"I'll take the helm, now, Demetri."

"He's slowing, too, skipper."

"Ahhhhh, to up-periscope and see a ship like mine is something of a shock to him, I reckon. He's curious, though.

"The Germans have commerce raiders, too. They probably look like this.

"No way he's going to surface now. No one would after seeing this. If he deviates the slightest bit, I'll stick to him like glue. That's probably what he's wanting to know. What do you think about this?"

"I think he might test you!" said Alexander as he stood watching the periscope through his binoculars.

"Dad, I think you're right! What do you think he'd do if we turned on him?"

"Well, mate, I hope he'd panic. He probably thinks we've got depth charges."

Alexei said, "Crash dive, friend. That be his best option."

"Hey, mate! Check out those Russians in uniform!"

"Some of my desperate passengers, friend. Remarkably interesting, Russian officers, a camouflaged ship, and no colours to be seen at all, just a house flag. They'd be having a good think about that?"

"The skipper would notice everything that's going on. Even that large crate down there. Don't armed merchantmen have an antiaircraft gun hidden in something like that?" asked George.

"Oh, yeah, they do. Interesting, George. I think we'll give him something more to think about," said Alexie.

"Yeah! Like?" asked Alexander.

"I'll show you. Demetri! Get three men to run down the starboard side and hide behind that crate. Tell them to stay there until I give the order to move the passengers away from the front of it. And call out to those Russian idiots to take cover. Ah, wave them away in full view of the periscope. No, don't wave them away, just call out."

"Aye, skipper!"

"The skipper would be saying, 'Hey, XO! What do you think about that?' He'd be worried," said Alexei.

"Yeah, mate, general quarters, do you reckon? I'd be worried about that crate, too."

"He'd probably be in two minds," said George.

"He wouldn't know what to think," said Alexander.

"Well, friend, whatever he's thinking, he'll need more time than we'll give him."

"Are you hoping he'll crash dive, mate?"

"I don't care what he does, friend, but he'll be doing something in a hurry. Be happy if he just goes away! Huh, I reckon my artwork is a good investment after all."

"Oh, yeah, it'd be interesting to see his stern reach

for the sky when he floods his forward ballast tanks," said Alexander.

"That'd be a good time to go for the rudder," said George.

"Now, you're with it, young George," said Grandpa.

"What about cavitation? Any cyclic stresses from repeated implosion?" asked Alexander.

"Hey? Oh, nah! I've only given her one good workout years ago to see how she went under rapid acceleration."

"That's good, the propellers won't fall apart when you give it to her, then?"

"Oh, no."

"Your hands are trembling again, skipper. I'll get you a coffee." He got a crew member to get everyone a coffee.

"If he goes rear up, mate, he'd be chasing the shallows to avoid hydrophone detection. Any around here where he can sit it out?"

Demetri said, "It's all too deep around here, besides, he won't be running for long.

"Around here isn't the right place to attack shipping."

"So, mate, he does a runner, expecting shock waves while he waits, nothing happening, he's worked it out we're full of bluff, and he comes after us like a shark in a feeding frenzy. How long before he's worked it out that we've been bluffing?"

"Well, it'd be good to have that foul weather here now. A quick turn, and if we keep her on cavitate, we should be able to lose him, and we'll have to keep a zig zag course, too."

"He'd be expecting us to make a move on him before that foul weather gets here," said Alexander.

"Maybe, he's waiting for it, too, mate?"

"Well, friend, he'd be wondering why we're not coming after him now. Well, the time to go for it is right now. He's not going to attack us."

"Let's get it over and done with!" said Alexander. He got the nod from the rest of the men.

Alexei gave a nod and said, "Demetri, tell the passengers to don life jackets when you've moved them away from the rails! Prepare for ramming!

"Feel the power when I give the cavitate bell, friends." He gave three blasts of the twelve-inch whistle and spun the helm hard a' starboard as soon as the propellers cherned the water.

"What's the whistle for, mate?"

"The custom is to alert the crew for action stations. I like to think this is my old battleship."

The ship vibrated violently from the extreme propeller cavitation, and passengers ran to the rails aft of the ship to see the mighty wake created by the powerful churning of the water. Crew members were powerless to prevent passengers from rushing to the rails on the port side and fore of the ship to secure a vantage point to view the spectacle.

Within seconds of the ship's turn to port, the sub's stern breached the surface dramatically. The water cascading from its outer hull and propellers offered a spectacular display. "What a sight. I thought he'd never go away," said Alexei.

"Oh, get us out of here! Quick!" asserted Alexander.

The ship's port bow just reached the spot where it looked as if it would strike the sub's stern as it disappeared beneath the surface. The sub's rudder was spared, but Alexei was happy just to make the thing go away.

A slight thud was felt with an eerie metal-to-metal groan that changed to a squeal echoing up from the depths.

"Didn't sound like we got the inner hull, Alexander."

"No, and it sounds like the outer hull might've been spared, too."

"Yeah, we'd better skedaddle and put some distance between us. Take the helm please, Demetri. Bring her around on bearing one zero six and keep her on cavitate. I'll organise a damage report."

"Phew, I'm glad that's over, mate!"

Demetri said, "Not over yet, Blue. No telling what he'll do. We could be watching a torpedo bare down on us. He's more likely to stay under, though. We just have to do frequent zig zag patterns and full power toward foul weather."

"Does it get confusing when you turn the helm to starboard and the ship turns to port, mate?"

"Only once in my greenhorn days. The lookout screamed, 'Obstacle on the port bow!' I spun her around 'hard a' starboard because it was the opposite to port, and I wanted to go in the opposite direction to the obstacle. Good thing I corrected it in time, though. Had an off day with no morning coffee. Anyway, I've never made that mistake again."

They conducted a visual sweep of the area through their binoculars.

Alexander, George, Grandpa, and Blue accompanied Alexei on deck, as he insisted on offering the passengers an explanation. When he confronted them, they cheered and yelled their approval. Something that he appreciated, but with typical modesty, he asserted that he was only doing his job and what was expected of him in their eyes.

One senior Russian naval officer commended him for his actions and encouraged others in giving him an honorary salute. He said, "Hip-hip-hip, hooray, hip-hip-hip, hooray, hip-hip-hip, hooray. Well done, captain."

"Thank you," he said and chatted to the passengers for a while.

Everyone on his ship knew that they were in good hands, but they knew that it was beneficial for all to keep a lookout for the enemy. No one was going to rest until dark, and they were hoping very much that the foul weather would stay all night.

Alexei organised a damage report and went straight back to relieve Demetri at the helm.

That night, Blue, George, and the Orloff family

gathered outside Alexander's cabin that was shared with Elizabeth, her husband, and their son, Alex.

"Dad, open up!"

"Hang on, George, wait till I find this confounded nuisance of a light switch to turn out the light. Where are you? Not used to this."

"She's nice and dark out here, mate. Could even get a bit of shuteye."

When the door was closed, Alexander flicked the light switch back on and squeezed past everyone to go to his bed to lie down. Alex followed him in and started asking questions about the day's events.

After about ten minutes, a banging noise was heard along with the sounds of squeaky springs coming from the cabin above. The seven-year-old young man was curious and asked, "What's that banging noise on the ceiling, Grandpa?"

"Good heavens! Ummmm, what noise?"

Blue heard the noise, too. He knew that Alex had put Alexander in a bit of a spot and said, "It sounds like they're having a pillow fight up there," hoping that it would satisfy his curiosity.

"Yes, it sounds like a bed, but the banging noise is getting too fast for it to be a pillow fight, Blue, and it's getting louder, in a rhythmic way. We didn't jump on the bed that fast when we had a pillow fight," he asserted, which made Alexander raise his eyeballs.

"Why can't it be? You ask too many questions, little

academic," asserted Alexander.

"What Blue said, Grandpa, there must be two of them, what are 'they' doing to the bed? It's getting faster," he persisted.

"Look! Give me that broom over there!" asserted Alexander.

He then grabbed the straw end of its handle close to the straw with both hands and lifted and pointed the other end of the handle at the ceiling. He then thrust the handle into the ceiling three times. And then, as if by magic, the knocking noise stopped abruptly.

"What were they doing, Grandpa?"

"Oh, I've got a terrible headache. I have to rest."

"What were they doing, Blue?"

"You should ask your father, mate."

"Where are you, Dad?"

"Hey, mate, do you want to know what my sister's dog gets up to at the station?" he said trying to put the 'bed episode' to bed.

Everyone tried to get in a position to be able to see him. Alexander had to share the single bed with the girls. There was standing room only for the rest of them. It was a perfect time to tell a couple of stories that would lighten the mood a bit.

"What breed is it, Blue?" asked Monica.

"He's a schnauzer, and he's a fat one at that. There's no 'kangaroo's short in his top paddock' with him. You see, he likes to fang into the good tucker.

"At the station, we give him roadkill until the general store gets the good bikkies in from the city. One day I picked up a sack of his favourites and left it on the floor of the kitchen while I went to unhitch the team from the wagon.

"When I got back, there he was. You guessed it, bikkies everywhere and one stuffed groaning canine.

"Mum and Lulu just came back from feeding the animals and had a good laugh after seeing him. Mum said, 'What do we do now?' Lulu said, 'You get the vet on the blower, Blue, and I'll give him some water.' When the switch put me through, and I explained everything, he said, 'Whatever you do, don't give him any water.' When I told them what they were shocked to learn, it was too late, he was no longer double in size. He resembled a small bail of the old golden fleece with sticks protruding from it. And he groaned so loud that there was no way I could hear myself think.

"The girls got hold of the old legs and took him to his day bed on the verandah. There was no way she was going to have a bar of him that night. They bunk together.

"Mate, do you think mum could get any sleep through the pathetic wailing that night, no way. 'What about a short nip of brandy with milk, that'll shut him up and make him sleep,' she said.

"They hit the sack with confidence, but minutes later, mum got out of bed. His snoring was much worse than his wailing, so they hunkered down in the barn for the night."

"What else does he get up to, Blue?" asked Monica.

He had a think. "When I take him to the beach, he usually sticks to me like a joey koala to its mum when in the water. This day was different, he was running amok. Why? He was checking out the local talent when he was supposed to be with me in the water. You see, he gets tired and needs a break now and then, so I hold him up out of the water for a bit. And when wet, he could even scare a scarecrow. He looks like a chimera or gargoyle with a big mo.

"When I was in the water, he lost sight of me. Yeah, girl dogs. I sang out to him, so he pushed on. When he got dumped by a wave, he started paddling towards another bloke who looked like me from behind. When he reached him, he scratched at his behind and grunted. The poor bloke thought his time was up. Everyone looked around when he screamed, but no one could make out what it was that frightened him. He just turned around and thrashed through the water to get to the beach. That bloke was the closest to get help from, so the poor dog kept after him.

"A huge wave picked the dog up and dumped him on the bloke's head. Boy, do you think he was going to release the headlock he put on the poor bloke? Huh, he screamed and thrashed like a girl trying to get away. Someone screamed, 'A killer seal has got him!'

And someone on the beach grabbed his rifle and ran for a better look as people in the water screamed and thrashed to get out.

"Everyone started laughing at the poor bloke when they heard my calls."

"He's not afraid to have a go, is he," said George.

"No, but you could call him a sook with attitude, mate. I got back to the station late one night when everyone was asleep. I thought I'd just make my way to my room in the dark instead of fumbling around trying to light the lantern. As soon as I opened the door, he started barking. He didn't know who I was, just kept his distance and barked.

"I slowly advanced with my arms up to feel my way in the dark, but I tripped on the rug and ran towards him while trying to regain my balance. Fair dinkum, the sook took off yelping up the hallway and ran into mum's room. Pathetic! He crawled under her bed and started barking again."

The mood lightened up a great deal, which was what everyone needed.

Monica and Blue exchanged smiles for everyone to see.

Mónica's hopes grew with every smile he gave her, and to him, she remained true.

Mary started to show a little more interest in Blue, too.

Eleven

Sub blasts merchant ship to smithereens

With so much going on, no one really had the time to reflect on the tumultuous period they were caught up in, and their concentration was centred on surviving the next leg of the voyage, which would put them in the waters of the war zone surrounding the British Isles.

Alexei enjoyed the company of his friends on the bridge every day. It was a particularly stressful time, as Alexei's ship could very well be blown out of the water by a mine or torpedo while heading for England, even with an escort.

Relief came when Alexei finally steamed up the Thames to the Port of London. "Here, we celebrate!" His passengers showed their gratitude by thanking God for their deliverance.

When docked, most of his passengers left the ship with the intention of staying, even though their passage was booked for other destinations. They were just so grateful to see land again.

There was concern of German Zeppelin attacks, and where night-time raiding was the norm, now people were expecting to be hit with a day-time raid, which was bound to happen sooner or later.

"My friends at the admiralty tell me that airships were bombing civilian houses unintentionally by being blown off course trying to bomb military targets. They're called 'baby-killers' because they killed a lot of babies," said Alexei.

Everyone stayed onboard the ship and engaged in discussions about German Zeppelin raids. "Are we safe here, Alexei?" asked George.

"Yeah, plenty of cloud and a good stiff breeze. We should sleep well, even on a clear night with a good breeze."

"They'd do better if they tried bombing the houses, mate."

"They can find their way to military targets in the dark, you know," said Alexei.

"Fair dinkum. How do they do that, mate?"

"They navigate their way by moonlight reflection on the Thames."

"Uncle Vladimir told me that a Zeppelin was shot down after it was lit up by searchlights. He fought with you in the Russo-Japanese War, is that right, Dad?"

"Yeah, another navy man. A very brave man, my brother."

"Ewwwww, I'd hate to be in one of those things and be shot at," said Monica.

Everyone was on deck looking skyward at the search lights scouring the night sky. The light show, while enthralling for some, was intimidating for the Hun.

Alexei wanted to get going as soon as business was taken care of, but there was no need for extra supplies thanks to the thinning out of his passengers, so there was no need to spend precious time looking around for something that was so hard to get hold of.

Alexei said, "Those Germans! Their long-range U-boat fleet is growing in number as we speak. They can stay at sea longer, too." He shook his head. "Nothing but trouble. When we get out of here, we won't be on their priority list, but they could just blast us out of the water so they could have the pleasure of saying, 'Well, that's one ship that'll never come back with supplies.' They're just trouble."

It was apparent that no one wanted to hear those words. No one said a word after that.

"Excuse me, Alexei."

"Yes, Vera."

"When you go to the port authority and see your friends in admiralty, could you ask them to track down Bill for me and give him this message? This is his name, rank, and serial number. I don't know where he is."

"Of course."

The next day, Alexei's friends were happy to oblige him and informed him of submarine activity in the area. He left the Thames to steam into the war zone bound for La Luz, his next port-of-call.

When he was on shore, Alexei befriended another ship's captain whose destination was the same as his, and they communicated with each other by way of electric lamp signalling to maintain radio silence as they travelled together. At night, they agreed not to signal, for obvious reasons. (Germans watching)

The voyage was free of incident since leaving England, but everything could change in an instant when coming into doubtful waters.

It was in and around the neutral territorial waters of the Canary Islands and surrounding archipelagos in the east central Atlantic, north-west of Africa, that German U-boat sightings were reported the previous week, and once again, all eyes scanned the ocean for periscope and smoke.

Before Germany's order of restricted submarine warfare, and since the resumption of unrestricted submarine warfare in the area, being the place where all trade routes to Europe from South America and the Cape of Good Hope converge, shipping was targeted by German U-boats. Their priority was to stop or slow all commerce bound for England.

Threatened British commerce interests in the islands necessitated the presence of the British navy. But that was of no great advantage to Alexei's mission. He said, "We want to be out of here pretty quick, for putzing around is a considerable health hazard."

The skipper of the other steamer mimicked Alexei's lead in frequently altering the speed of each leg of the zigzag course, even though the practice would put a considerable strain on his coal reserves, of which he, too, kept a good supply.

Around midday, approaching an area known for German U-boat activity close to their destination, the lookouts sounded the alarm bells and screamed, "Smoke! Dead ahead!"

"Signal the other…, nah, he's seen it, too! Sound general quarters!" The crew was disciplined and trained by the man they loved, for it was of mutual benefit that his ship be run with the precision of a navy ship. But instead of manning the guns, they manned the fire hoses.

There was complete harmony and order when everyone worked together and communicated as a team on his ship, and there may not have been any threat, but Alexei was prudent after fighting many a battle, and it was better to be ready for the unknown.

"Three smoke plumes, now!"

"A convoy?" queried Alexander.

"It looks like it. It's a good thing I told my friend to

make sure he got someone to communicate my description, and that I'm a friendly, to the fleet commander operating in this area." He wanted no problems.

"British?" queried Alexander.

"Yes, haaaaaaaaa. Signal this for confirmation," he told his signaller, reading the blinker message (lamp signalling) through his binoculars after the destroyer messaged him. "Ask him if there's any U-boat threat?"

"No, you're safe," said the signaller.

"Yeah, mate, we're safe but they're not."

Alexei said, "Yeah, a destroyer could only mean one thing."

"Munitions?" queried George.

Alexei said, "Yeah, they'll be in trouble sooner or later."

"They'd have to work together with that many ships," said Grandpa.

"Good heavens, yeah, Dad. They 'hit and run' like wolves. Just two could do a lot of damage. One takes out the straggler and sits on the bottom in shallow water. The other hits the lead ship while the destroyer is doing a search. Unable to find that sub, it chases after the other one. There's not much the skipper can do because they can escape hydrophone detection by sitting on the bottom where they can't get a reading."

The last ship, the straggler, was about three hundred yards behind the convoy. Most of the passengers had already been viewing the convoy, half a mile off Alexei's starboard beam, from the rails since the smoke was sighted.

"Mate, they're heavy ships! I'd hate to be on any one of those."

"Shit!" screamed Alexei as the straggler disappeared with one very loud cataclysmic explosion. Large chunks of the ship's burning superstructure hurtled skyward with a massive plume of black smoke.

A moment after the blast, Alexei screamed, "Take cover!" Huge chunks of metal from the disintegration splashed down on and near the ship.

The ship it was following caught fire from burning debris that crashed onto its deck.

As soon as Alexei realised what was going on, he immediately called the emergency teams into action. The toughest of men cowered as steel crashed on deck and shattered windows. "Demetrius! Have those fires put out and have someone check to see if there are any wounded or dead. Get the passengers to help with that, too, please.

"George! Go and check on the family…"

"Fire on that ship!" screamed a passenger.

"You haven't been hit, have you, mate?"

"Heavens! I can't feel any broken bones, but that chunk of steel could have killed someone."

Alexei put the E.O.T. handle to full steam ahead and ported his helm to steer the ship to starboard immediately.

"You, men! Get that man down to the ship's doctor, please! Could you passengers check on other people who maybe injured?" screamed Demetrius as he gave the orders to the other crew members and passengers.

"Roll out the fire hoses and make ready the pumps, Demetrius! Get the nets ready in case they abandon ship!"

"That fire is spreading pretty fast, mate."

"Yeah," said Alexei.

"Only one bad one, no crew injured, skipper," Demetrius reported.

"Good. Thank you. Lifeboat team stand by with hammers!" he yelled.

The destroyer deviated and was in hot pursuit of the sub.

Looking through his binoculars, Alexei said, "It looks like his priority is the sub, not the burning ship. It's up to us." He turned the E.O.T. handle to half speed as he approached the ship on its starboard side. "Fix high-pressure hoses and start the pumps! Stand by to open valves!" he ordered.

The water from the six powerful hoses engulfed the major fires as his ship came alongside. "Full speed astern!" he ordered. (to stop the ship.)

Part of the troubled ship's crew, mainly those who were unable to help or who were getting in the way of the emergency teams, had been ordered to abandon ship as Alexei's ship came to a stop.

When the destroyer was in full pursuit of the sub, Alexei knew that there was little chance of his ship being blown out of the water by a sub because of the direction the destroyer was headed. There was also the uncertainty of knowing where the other sub was, that is, if there were two subs. Another explosion would confirm that there were two.

A U-boat skipper would not waste a torpedo on Alexi's unladen ship to get to the troubled ship with the possibility of giving away his position and have a destroyer bearing down on him. He would wait and see or concentrate his efforts elsewhere, or he would just lie on the bottom. It was too risky for an attack on the distressed ship, as the destroyer was still in the vicinity where the sub would have to take up a firing position on the distressed ship, leaving it with little time to be able to escape.

Alexei could get to the ship and fight fires without worrying. Still, he had no idea what the ship was carrying, but he had a good idea. Despite the danger, he and his crew selflessly helped in a situation that looked as though it could have been a futile but deadly attempt.

All fires were extinguished just minutes after the destroyer disappeared into the black smoke plume that was about to engulf the convoy.

The men in the water were getting into the lifeboats that Alexei had lowered for them, as some men jumped ship before their lifeboats had been filled and lowered from their ship.

Communication was finally established between the skippers and crew. The okay was given to Alexei that the ship was secure after a thorough damage report and inspection was conducted. The men who were ordered to abandon ship made their way back onboard their ship.

Alexei said to the men, "All those onboard the doomed ship didn't know what hit them and had no time to suffer, and it's ironic that, through their demise, they'd give protection to the rest of the convoy in one final act of mateship. Through that thick black smoke following the ships, the enemy would have too much trouble finding them to attack. They go with the wind. We salute you, fellow mariners. Let's have two minutes silence."

Before Alexei ported his helm to resume his original course, he conducted a search of the waters around where the burning hull sank. There was a lot of smouldering debris just visible in the smoke but no sign of life or death.

The skipper of the troubled ship admitted to Alexei that he was about to order the rest of the crew to abandon ship, but he resigned from doing so when Alexi's fire hoses extinguished the flames they were battling.

Alexei resumed a zigzag course, but he, like everyone onboard, would remain prudent until they reached land, even though the last leg of the voyage was considered safe.

Though sick with apprehension about family left behind, curiosity of their new home prompted the families to ask questions of Blue and concentrate on building a new life instead of worrying themselves sick. Monica asked, "What are we getting ourselves into, Blue?"

"Well, nothing much. Wide open spaces, hot weather, cold weather, snow and ice, lots of water, drought, and opportunities for everyone. You can get burnt out, drowned, eaten, stung to death, die from a snake bite, or fried alive. Just the usual."

"Oh, really?" queried George.

"What sort of creatures are you talking about, Blue?"

"Humans, Vera. No, just joking. Box jellyfish, sharks, crocodiles. ah, too many deadly snakes and spiders to name. I could go on for yonks. Just got to watch your step. Deadly funnel-web spiders love to make their home in your boots while you sleep, and snakes catch vermin in the chook pen.

"I saw an eastern brown slither up behind my then wife who was bent over weeding her flower garden. It went straight between her legs and onto the patch that she was weeding. Fair dinkum, when she saw it, she leapt in the air backwards from the bent position and did a complete about face before she hit the ground. Then she leapt out of there like a kangaroo.

"Even the cat looks carefully before jumping over long grass. A mate was walking through long grass to get to the river when he stepped on a snake. It struck him just above the ankle. Fair dinkum, the fangs got stuck in his leggings, which he religiously wore with his boots every day. He shook his leg trying to free it as he ran crying and screaming, poor bugger. It stayed with him all the way home, though."

"Heck, they don't come inside the house, do they?"

"Just don't let the cats in. They seek your phrase by bringing to you their best executed catch-of-the-day gift, usually a deadly snake, and it's just about always alive when it's dropped at your feet."

"Ewahhhh," said Monica.

"One day, Graeme, the station cat, so named because of his grey fur, came inside with his catch when a wedding reception was under way. Mate, there was a blood-curdling scream that made a few hardened drovers drop their beer. It dropped a snake in the middle of a group of people."

"That would've been interesting," said George.

"What happened then, Blue?" asked Monica.

"Well, can you imagine people running in all directions and screaming as they leapt over furniture and clambered through windows as they were bumping into each other? The poor snake was just as terrified as the guests were. I reckon, if it slithered away, the place would've been completely trashed. The poor thing just froze and looked around."

"Well, it's a good place to live if you know what's going on, right?" said Vera.

"Look, it's just a matter of getting to know and respect the place."

"My coal reserves are running a bit low, Alexander. I'll have to do the last leg without zig-zag."

"Ok, I'll get my lot out with binoculars."

"Thanks, the rest of the passengers will do the same."

That night, Blue was getting excited about being home soon.

Monica lay awake thinking of the times that she and Blue shared.

Mary was making a move on Blue every opportunity she had, which made him think, "When she said, 'Goodnight, Blue.' What was that all about? But it was the way she said it."

Twelve

Blue and the nobles reach Australia

When Alexei brought his ship into the Port of Brisbane, there was a big sigh of relief.

The arrangement was for Blue to contact the station to announce their arrival, so that his men could bring two trucks to Brisbane to pick them up the next day.

They stayed the night in Brisbane after spending the rest of the day and the next morning sorting out customs and immigration issues for Australian permanent residency.

The previous year's torrential rain that fell in the area of Blue's property near Roma, west of Brisbane, made the grass grow tall and turn to ground fuel (dry grass) over winter. There was too much for livestock to keep it down. The potential for a brushfire to materialise over the summer months was great, but somehow, the area escaped disaster after having been subjected to several weeks of extremely high temperatures.

The dusty drive in the truck on an unseasonably hot day in late March reminded Blue of the coldies he enjoyed at the local pub after a hot day working the property.

"I hope you put enough in the fridge, mate?" Blue asked Ted as he and George bounced around on the ripped leather bench seat of the old workhorse with the driver waiting for his answer.

"Ah, mate, I forgot."

"Yeah, right, Ted! Ask a stupid question, get a stupid answer.

"Plenty of ground fuel there, mate? Did the livestock get the grass down all the way to the creek from the station house?"

"Yeah, good firebreak, now. I gave the blokes overtime to move them (cattle) around all summer."

Blue said, "Big bushfire threat here, George."

"Hold on!" shouted old Ted as he slammed on the brakes and gripped the steering wheel.

"What's that?" asked George.

The truck skidded on the dirt road after two kangaroos had crossed safely to the other side of the road in front of him.

"Why don't you keep going?" asked George as the truck continued to skid.

"Hurry up!" said Ted as the huge herbivores suddenly changed direction and hopped back onto the road when they were startled by the truck.

"That's why, mate," said Blue as one slammed into the front of the truck's bumper.

"Oh, okay."

"He's having a sticky beak under the truck, and he's too big to pull out. That big pothole up ahead will do the job. Hang on!"

"Well, that's what they do, mate. They're so unpredictable that you just have to expect a hit, and where there's one, there's a lot more," said Ted.

Ted drove the truck over the pothole after Blue got out.

"He's free!" shouted Blue.

"The potholes are deep!" said George.

Ted said, "The corrugation is worse, mate.

"Okay, mate, can you give us a hand please?" looking at George as he got out of the truck.

George asked, "Are you going to drag him off the road?" Everyone piled out of the trucks to observe a new experience. It was all new to them.

"No, mate, we're going to tie him to the front bar."

George thought he was having a dig at him and laughed.

"Good dog food, mate," said Ted as the three men heaved it on the bar.

George was taking it all in, as he was interested in learning as much as possible. He said, "You know how to drive."

"Well, I learnt the hard way, you just don't swerve to avoid a roo on the frog n' toad (kangaroo on the road) full of potholes. A quick way to the gates, (pearly gates) mate, and they all come out to feed on the grass every day around dusk."

The girls had never seen a kangaroo before, and they were a bit upset to have seen a dead one. They studied it well before getting back into the truck.

"Wow! What's that running across the road?" asked George.

"An emu," said Ted as he sounded the klaxon.

"Oh, I've heard of them but never seen one."

When the trucks drove over the stock grid on the road to the station house at dusk, the girls caught sight of familiar faces in the distance outside the house. They stood in the back of the truck holding on to the wooden rails looking over the cab waving and calling out as the klaxons sounded repeatedly.

The blue heelers (dogs) ran up to greet them and

barked their welcome at the newcomers until they were competing with family for attention at the house.

The family swamped the trucks to greet them, but Vera avoided her mother.

Natty ran up to Blue with a gift for him and was so excited that she ran straight past her sisters without acknowledging them. She said, "I missed you so much, and this is something I did just for you."

"Oh, thank you, Natty. A painting?"

"Yeah, and that's us," she said as she pointed to the figures that were holding hands with the words 'I love you' written on top.

"Oh, how sweet," he said and curiously looked at her.

"Come and have a look at my school bag." She took him by the hand and led him away leaning forward as she strained to pull his arm. He turned and smiled at the others as he was led away.

Monica just stood and watched, and deep down she knew that she had a job on her hands to be one step ahead of her rivals.

Without waiting to be cautioned by management for their colourful language around the station, the men voluntarily toned it down and restricted their shenanigans to the confines of their accommodation and firepit, both of which were situated some distance from the house.

What little the men knew about etiquette, they made up for by being worthy of the respect that was shown to them by the new Australians who embraced them like they were family.

The killer (a beast to be slaughtered for station hands consumption) that was bled for days and left roasting over the firepit, was ready to be served up.

"Thank God you're all safe, we were so worried when we heard news of the revolution," said Natasha.

"Heavens, it was a nightmare! So worried about Vladimir and Fiona and the family. I hope they're safe and that they stuck to their back up plan.

"It's still upsetting not knowing why they failed to turn up, though."

Natasha asked, "I wonder what they're going to do with Nicki and Alexandria? And what about the poor children? We only know that they're under house arrest."

"Nickolas can go to hell as far as I'm concerned. I hope they give him what he dished out. If they do, no one will see him again. I Just feel sorry for the kids because they were brainwashed! It's taken so much out of me, losing everything," said Grandpa as he was helped to a bench seat while everyone studied his words for a while.

Ted showed sympathy before he told the guests that he would show them to their rooms. The deafening screeching of a large flock of sulphur-crested cocka-toos and the sight of hundreds of huge red kangaroos hopping past in the paddocks nearby captivated the new Australians. They were in awe of the country's diverse wildlife splendour, and it helped a bit to take an emotional break from the recent adverse circumstances.

Blue was spared the trouble of making the guests comfortable, as that was already taken care of. They were told to fang in when large platters of tender succulent beef steaks and baked vegetables were brought to the table.

"What do you think of the beef?" asked Blue.

Everyone was too busy gorging themselves to stop and answer. They just nodded their approval.

"Hicck, itzz tnisssuissenderr," George mumbled through a big mouthful.

"He said it's tender," said Vera.

"Yeah, it wasn't stressed when it went. Ta-ta, so to speak," said Ted.

"I love the fire you've got going," said Vera.

"Yeah, it gets a bit cool out here at night," said Blue.

Natty said, "We've been making damper, Vera. We made it, and Uncle Ted put it in the camp oven to cook. It was lovely with butter and jam when it was hot, but it was like eating rubber when it cooled down. Do you want some? And I'm going to school."

"Oh, yeah. What's a damper, then? And what's a camp oven?"

"Well, the pioneer's damper was flour, water, and a pinch of salt kneaded and thrown on the hot coals of their campfire. That was their bread. A camp oven is a cast iron pot with a lid that they cooked it in over the fire," said Blue.

"Oh, I'll definitely have to give it a go, then."

"I didn't want to give the girls my recipe because it's got beer in it. Extra rise from the bubbles," said Ted.

"Wow, the night sky is so clear! You can see the Milky Way," said George.

"What's that noise?" asked Monica.

"Cicadas and green frogs, there's a lot of them, and they all talk to each other. They're noisy little creatures, especially before the roosters start doing their thing when it's still," said Blue.

After having slept in, the family woke to greet the new day with a little less stress but not without concern for their loved ones in Russia.

The chirping of rainbow lorikeets in the trees, the roosters crowing, the grinding metal squeaks of the windmill blades, and the cracking of whips and commands shouted at the cattle that echoed through their bedroom, was having a calming effect on them, and it was a very new experience that they were becoming fond of.

They were greeted by Blue as they emerged. He asked, "Bacon and eggs with coffee, Alexander?" as he prepared breakfast for all his guests.

"Oh, yes please. I haven't forgotten the last time I had this." His eyes followed the plate to the table.

"Good morning," said Adelaide as she emerged yawning.

Blue said, "They got up with the roosters, and the

blokes have given them something to think about.

"Who wants to gather eggs with me after brekky?"

Natty said, "Make sure there's no 'Jo Blakes' under the chooks."

"Huh?" queried Monica.

"Jo Blakes! Who are they?" asked Alexander.

"Snakes," said Natty.

"Snakes hide under the chooks?" queried Alexander.

Cliff, a station hand, just walked into the kitchen to talk to Blue and overhead the conversation about the eggs, and being a character, he thought it was a perfect opportunity to impress the Orloff girls.

He had only just found a dead snake the previous day and left it in the meat safe to use for fish bait. He thought, "If I put the dead snake under a chook, I can pretend to find it and tell them, 'This is how you catch a live snake!' When I lift the chook a little, I'll see it and tell them, 'Oh, look, a snake!' Then I'll make out that it's still alive, a little shake will make it look real. After I show them, they'll be impressed, and then I can run outside with it. They'll never know it was dead. Walla, Cliffie the hero. They'll love me.

"Yeah, that's what I'll do. Good idea, Cliffie, you hero, you."

He was in the chook pen when everyone turned up and had already put the dead snake under a chook. "G'day, I'm Cliff, I was just checking the pen for snakes," he said, which made the girls nervous and prompted them to look around.

Blue was with them, and before Cliff even opened his mouth, he knew that the character was up to something, as he only carried on the way he did to impress someone. He said, "What are you up to, Cliff?"

"What are you talking about, boss? I just wanted to make sure there were no snakes in here so the girls would be safe."

"What! You and snakes?"

Cliff tried to shut his boss up and said, "I'm not afraid of snakes! I play with them all the time."

"Oh, right," Blue said and turned to the girls. "I'll tell you how much he likes snakes. He was sitting on a chair having lunch one day with his lunch box at his feet as he always does in the shade under a tree near the bush. When he was eating a sandwich, a brown snake slithered under his chair and was at his lunch box when he reached down to get another one.

"When he saw it, he threw his hand skywards and from the sitting position, he did a double backflip with a twist and hit the ground running, screaming until he got to his room…"

"No, that was someone else!"

Ted was outside and called out, "Boss, can you help me here for a bit?"

Cliff seized his opportunity when Blue went outside and said, "Hang on, I better just check this one. Oh, look, there's one."

Everyone strained to see as he reached for its tail, but the girls started to get worried and voiced their concerns loudly.

Blue came back after he heard Monica yell, "Be careful, Cliff!"

Natty and Mary ran past Ted at the doorway as he, too, came running when he heard Monica.

Blue saw the tail, but before he could say or do anything, Cliff pulled the snake out from beneath the chook and lifted it up for everyone to see. He was going to shake it, but it started to thrash around by itself in his hand. When he realised it was alive, he screamed and threw it at the family before running out.

Alexander was bent over backwards thrashing his arms about trying to hit it away from him and wacked it towards George, who, having a fear of snakes, threw his arms back and did a dance with several kicks and hops before leaping for the door.

"It didn't bite you, did it, mate?" asked Ted.

"Oh, I hope not!" he said as he checked himself while making his way outside.

Cliff was so embarrassed that he went and hid while Ted caught the snake.

He checked the pen before the girls cautiously gathered the eggs.

On the way back, Ted said, "A snake got inside a neighbour's place, and the silly bugger tried to kill it with a shovel when it was cornered, but he was struck three times in the hand before he could thrust the shovel an inch toward it. He died soon after."

"Good heavens, that quick?"

"Yeah, mate, when they're cornered, they're super quick. He should've just left the front door open and waited for it to come out."

"How many snakes are there around here?" asked Vera.

"Well, you're not stepping over them all the time, but be careful around piles of tin and wood, and of course, around the chook pen where vermin hang out."

When back at the house, they sat in the kitchen. "G'day, I'm Charlie, the cook. You must be Vera?"

"Yes, pleased to meet you, Charlie. The beef was beautiful and tender. And the flavour, how'd you do that?"

Blue said, "Charlie's one of the best when it comes to creating ways to cook something that'll satisfy the men. The men booted the last cook out."

"Thanks, boss. Gum leaves, Vera. Just break off a branch and chuck it in the fire to smoke anything you like. To get the flavour you want, just get a leaf, scrunch it, smell it, and keep going until you get the one with the smell you like."

"It's amazing how there's no end to the possibilities in cooking, is there, Charlie?"

"Yeah, a bit of 'bush nounce'."

"I reckon, mate," said Vera, trying to assimilate the

Australian lingo with a slight Russian accent.

"Well, I'm impressed, you sound like one of us already," he said with a surprised look.

The sisters who came to the station first were familiar with everyone and gave their siblings some insight into how the men felt about them. Macca, whose youth threatened the older men's chances in the arena of romance, was one of just a handful of young men left in the area, as many others, local and countrywide, swamped the recruitment centres to join the army to fight for king and country. The rush to volunteer for service had declined dramatically, though, since word got back from the trenches in Gallipoli of the high casualty rate there.

Monica stayed true to Blue, even though the young jackaroo, Macca, had his eyes on her since she arrived.

That night, Blue lay in bed thinking of Natty. He thought, "What a beautiful thing that was she did for me, but it's what the painting suggests that worries me. What is it with these girls?"

Thirteen

Blue and his friends make two rescues

After the families settled in for a few weeks, the sky was dark green in the west, a sign of hail. Fortunately, Blue's men had already left with the herd days earlier when the mare's tail clouds were noticed. The cattle drive to the yards in town, where storms usually bypass, required a mammoth effort and only took seven days to accomplish.

"Do you get many storms around here, Blue?" asked George.

"Yeah, mate, always predictable. We've got to batten down the hatches. Help me move those two tables close to the fireplace, mate. I'll grab some cushions for everyone to sit on under the tables."

"Wow, is it going to be that bad when everything has

to be tied down?"

"Yeah, things take off around here, mate, but it only lasts ten minutes, thank goodness."

"Will we be safe, Blue?" asked Natty.

"Yeah, of course, the two brick fireplace chimneys anchor the place down. Which reminds me, I want to check on the Carters after the storm. A couple of oldies down the track. There's a widow maker close to their house."

"That's the tree you were telling us about?"

"That's the one. Extremely dangerous."

"Ah, I'm getting too old for this," said Grandpa as he had to be helped down under the table.

"Here, rest against this, Dad." Alexander piled cushions behind him.

A terrifying thunderclap made everyone jump just after the strong smell of rain. Both Monica and Natty grabbed hold of Blue's arms and held on tight as they cowered in terror under the table.

There was a crash on the corrugated iron roof, then another, and more and more large chunks of hail battered the roof until it became a constant pounding with deafening results.

The flash of lightning that preceded the deafening thunderclaps gave them warning, and Blue kept an eye on the walls for any sign of movement, which would tell him if the house was going fall apart by the howling gales outside.

Soon, Monica had her arms around Blue's waist and her head under his arm, and she was hoping that the storm would last all night. The others were cowering as they watched the walls for the reflection of lightning.

Within a couple of minutes, torrential rain replaced the hail, and the thunder moved away to frighten other people and animals in its path.

Everyone converged on the back verandah and marvelled at a wild afternoon. The awesome power and diversity of nature never ceased to amaze anyone who witnessed it.

The treetops and a large flock of screeching sulphur-crested cockatoos were brightly illuminated by the sun which shone from blue skies and contrasted them dramatically against the storm's black wake.

The once-browned landscape, which was turned into an icy plain in five minutes, was left riddled with uprooted trees and broken branches.

"The lines are down, and I can't get through to the switch.

"George! Come with me to check on the Carters. We'll go in the rain because I've got a feeling we should go now."

"Yeah, ok."

"Nikolai and I will do a check of the house and look after the girls," said Alexander.

"Thanks, mate."

"Can I come, Blue?" asked Monica.

"Oh, I don't know."

"Pleeeeeeeease."

"Only If It's okay with your dad."

"Okay, but don't make a nuisance of yourself. Do you understand?"

"I won't, Papa."

Donned in oilskin gear and broad-brimmed hats, the three men ran to the barn where Blue threw a couple of axes and a crowbar in the back of the truck before driving off down the track.

"This road sure is slippery!" said George.

"Look! What's that?" shouted Monica.

"It's a blue flyer, a female red kangaroo," said Blue.

"Osphranter rufus!" (red kangaroo) said Alexander. "I've been studying up."

"It's sitting on its tail!" said George.

"It'd be six-foot high, easy," said Monica.

"What's that sticking out of its tummy?" asked Monica.

"It's her little hopper. (joey) Head jammed between its legs," said Blue. "They go to the pouch up until they're twelve months old, and they're quite a bundle for mum to haul around, too."

The large troop that hopped across the road behind the kangaroo took a minute to clear the way, such was their number.

After a while, the house was in view as they bounced and slid around in the old truck in the slushy corrugation of the road.

As they drove into the property, Blue's fears were confirmed when they saw that a huge branch from a massive gum tree near the house had come down on the roof.

No one was sure if anyone was injured or trapped inside.

"Grab the axes, George! You stay in the truck, Monica!"

"I can hear you!" shouted Blue as he responded to the screams for help.

"We're trapped!" screamed the male occupant as his wife confirmed that they were both okay.

"Are you near the door?"

"No!"

Blue busted the door's lock with one blow of the axe and gained entry.

"There's a lot of rubble blocking the door access, but you can get through the brick wall to your left of the door. Are you able to smash through it?"

"Yeah, we'll get you out, mate."

With the crowbar, they were through in no time.

"Oh, thank you so much." The elderly lady was unscathed as she crawled out.

"Oh, I'm so glad you happened to come by." The man gave his rescuers a big handshake.

Hank and Jill were escorted to the truck by Monica before introductions were made.

"Any animals need rescuing, mate?"

"No, they should be okay because the pen's still standing."

"No broken bones?"

"No, thankfully."

"Okay, come and stay with us until we get this sorted out."

"Sorted out? We've got no money."

"She's right, mate. We'll do the worrying about that. We'll fix your place for nothing."

"You'll do that for us out of the kindness of your heart?"

"Mate, if you can't help a neighbour in trouble, you're not all there."

When the rain eased up, Blue asked, "Monica, can you and George ride in the back on the way home, please?"

"Oh, no! That's unacceptable! Noooooooooooooooo, not me, this is my spot, next to you my love, and nothing is going to change my mind. Get Them to sit in the back!" Monica thought before she said, "Sure."

The landscape was still white with hail as Blue drove home carefully on the slushy road.

"Someone up there sure is looking after you, mate, I had a strong feeling to come. The whole tree should've come down in that storm.

"A young girl was killed at her school by a widow maker. It was a fine day, too."

The couple looked at him, and when he stopped talking, they looked at him intently.

"Ah, sorry, I get passionate about these things. To think that someone who's only just starting out in life is whacked. It's not fair! It makes me sick, too."

"That makes sense," said Hank.

When Blue got back to the station, Monica was surprised that he showed her the courtesy of helping her down from the back of the truck. It afforded her great pleasure, and she instinctively knew that her efforts were coming to fruition. She also knew that it was only a matter of time before great love and happiness would befall them as a couple.

Charlie went with the herd to feed the men, so Vera decided to start preparing the mince and union filling for a pile of pirozhki pies to serve up for dinner.

Blue walked in with his guests and said, "Oh, yeah! I know that smell anywhere, and I hope you made plenty?"

"Ah, stone the crows, mate! I forgot to allow for you," she said, still practicing her Australian slang.

"Ah, you make joke, da? Ha, ha, you funny person," he said, affectionately mocking her with a Russian accent.

"No!"

"Now I'm worried. It looks like my larrikin sense of humour has finally rubbed off on you."

After introductions, the couple was made to feel

welcome when hot coffee was offered to them while they dried off around the fire.

The next day, Blue left a note on the door of the men's quarters notifying them of the work to be done at the at their neighbour's place.

The men spent most of the day chopping the huge branch into manageable pieces and cleaning up. They were told to stop and enjoy a cup of tea and scones that the women had baked in a camp oven over hot coals for them. A beef stew and vegetables had been simmering for hours in a large camp oven hanging on a tripod chain over another fire.

As the men were about to resume work, two truck-loads of men arrived with carpentry tools and timber.

"We've timed it well, it looks like all the hard work's been done, mate," said Ted as he buckled his tool belt that was loaded with everything to do the job.

He was a builder long ago but still knew his stuff. "No one's allowed to come in here until I give the ok!"

"Stew's ready! Come and get it!" called Adelaide. The girls ladled it out in enamelled tin plates and gave them hot coffee in matching cups.

"It's not that bad, mate. Only one damaged truss. We'll get stuck into it tomorrow." The American couple handed him a plate of stew and damper.

Everyone did well to finish the job in two weeks. A satisfying accomplishment.

A dark sky was looming, and there was no way they

were going to be cut off by a swollen creek.

"We can't thank you enough. We've never experienced kindness like this before," said Jill.

"Well, you can always help someone else if they need it."

"Yes." They looked at him deep in thought. "Thank you, everyone," said Jill.

"Yeah, thanks everyone," said Hank.

To avoid getting drenched, everyone had to run for the station house when they got back in the pouring rain that was quickly setting in.

"God bless you and everyone who helped," said Hank.

"They know what it's like, they've been there, mate."

"Lord knows I'm beginning to understand a little better, Blue," said Alexander.

"That calls for a beer then, mate."

"No, more like a couple!"

"Oh, Blue, I love you so much, please kiss me? No, will you marry me? And you better not tell me about your being too old for me. That's got nothing to do with love. Do you know how hard it is for a girl to find a real man like you? You do love me, don't you?" thought Monica as she sat and fantasised, her eyes not leaving him for a second.

The next day, Blue said to Ted, "I've got that feeling again, mate."

"What now, mate?"

"Got to go to town."

"You know the ford will be flooded until tomorrow."

"Yeah, mate, but if I don't listen, I pay."

Everyone, including the women, piled into the truck and headed for town. When they reached the ford, it was flooded.

"Is that a car in the tree?" queried George.

"Yeah, mate! Let's go!"

"Anyone in it?" asserted Alexander as they searched on the run.

"Quiet, I thought I heard something!" asserted Blue.

"Over there!" said Ted.

"My son! Please find my son!" shouted the man as he sobbed while clinging to a tree branch in the water.

"George! Help him to the truck." They scurried across rocks and branches down the edge of the swollen creek.

"He was washed away! How stupid of me!" he shouted before he cried.

"We'll find him!" George left him with the girls and ran off.

"He's only fifteen!" Vera put her hand on his shoulder and prayed.

After twenty minutes of searching, those at the truck heard shouting. The man stopped sobbing and stood before he optimistically focused his attention on the group in the distance.

"He's okay!" shouted Blue.

The man ran to his son and embraced him.

"Oh, Mike, my boy, I'm so sorry. Thank God! That was such a stupid thing I did!"

"It's okay, Dad, I'm fine. Something strange happened. I was ready to give up, but I suddenly got a boost of strength. I was weak as a kitten. Weird."

"Yeah? Well, I'm thankful for that, that's for sure.

"It didn't look that threatening, and the water wasn't that deep! It didn't wash me away when I walked through it to check it out."

"Well, mate, fast-running water going through your legs is a lot different to it pushing up against a car."

"I won't be doing that again, that's for sure. Being a day late is better than not coming back at all. Now I'm really embarrassed, and grateful."

"Ah, better to be embarrassed and learn from it than to be sorry, mate.

"Stay with us tonight, and we'll come back for your car tomorrow."

"Thanks, Blue."

"She's right, mate. We all find out the hard way.

"Next time you're out here, ask the locals what's going on. They want to help. One good word of advice, though, when you drive over the crest of a hill, slow down, anything could be on the other side."

"That's advice I'll never forget, and I'll put it into practice, too."

After introductions at the station, Blue invited Bill

and Mike to have dinner with everyone and made them comfortable.

Cliff said, "Are ya from the 'big smoke' (city) or something, mate?"

"Nar, come off it, mate, with a 'bag of fruit' (suit) like that, he'd have to work at the sheep station forking hay," said Ted.

"Yeah?"

"No." Ted shook his head.

"Cliff is our best 25-year-old station hand."

"Yes, I'm a barrister from the Gabba," said Bill, who got a smile from Ted.

"A what, from the where?" queried Cliff.

"I practice law, and I have an office at Woolloongabba, in Brisbane."

"Practice? How long do ya have ta practice it for before you're really good at it?"

"Hey?" said Bill.

"You idiot, it's 'called' a practice. He already does it!

"It's okay, mate, he was raised with the dingoes in the bush," said Ted.

"Where's the Gabba?" asked Cliff.

Ted said, "Well, do you know where the abattoir is in Brisbane, mate?"

"Yeah, I know where that is."

"Well, it's nowhere near that."

"Well, that's helpful, mate! Thanks," he said as he shook his head.

"That'll teach you for building my hopes up the other day. I asked him if he'd seen my vest, to which he replied, 'Describe it.' I said, 'It's brown steerhide with a white patch.' He said, 'Ohhhhhhhhh, the brown steer hide vest with a white patch?' hinting that he knew where it was, and naturally I was excited, but then he said, 'Nah, haven't seen it.' Get some of your own back.

"How'd you go at the pub last night, anyway, Cliff?"

"Just the usual. A bunch of blokes attacked another bunch of blokes with cricket bats."

"why didn't they go armed with their own cricket bats?"

"Huh?"

"Well, would you go taking on a bunch of blokes wielding bats?"

"No! The blokes with bats attached another bunch of blokes."

"Oh, I see. Another boring night at the pub, then?"

"Well, Bill, you and Mike are still alive," said Blue.

"Yeah, this has opened my eyes, well and truly," said Bill as he held his son.

"Well, mate, I only drive as fast as I would to be able to stop within the distance from where I am on the road, to the point where the road ahead is unclear. The rule I live by now.

"While I'm at it, young Cliff, you're in big trouble!"

"What have I done now, boss?"

"You haven't been listening! How many times have

I told you how to drive the tractor? I saw you driving it diagonally down the hill the other day. A good way to roll it, mate! And you know that it could roll on top of you. We hear about it all the time.

"Also, watch out for the ruts in the track down there. When you hit them front on, the tractor will bounce, won't it? Yeah, you know all about It, so why do you keep doing it? Diagonally across the tracks, not the hill, mate!"

The next day, when the floodwaters subsided, Blue took the men to the creek and recovered the car. On the roadside, they checked its petrol tank for water contamination. The rotor button in the distributor was dried and the carburettor was dismantled and flushed before the engine was cranked.

New friendships were formed, and Bill was alerted to the hazards of kangaroos on the road, mainly around dusk and around dawn but also during the day.

Fourteen

Two sisters in love with Blue

Natty was getting upset at the way Monica was chasing after Blue all the time. She complained regularly to her mother that she was being teased by her, and that she told her that Blue lost interest in her. As a result, she would mope around with depression. She was depressed enough over her inability to get her parents to accept her committing to Blue, about which he knew nothing.

When Monica was approached by her mother with Natty at her side, insisting on a settlement between the two, Natasha was adamant that she was not about to allow the issue to continue to disrupt their attentiveness when studying.

"G'day, Natasha. Why's Natty looking so glum, today?"

"She's always glum. I'm afraid it's got to do with you, Blue."

"Yeah?"

"She and Monica think that they're in an advanced stage of their upbringing. They think that they can concentrate on matters of the heart instead of finding time to study, and I'm afraid you're the one they've got their sights set on."

"Oh, they've got their sights set on me?"

"I love you, Blue. I love you so much," said Natty.

He stood utterly dumbfounded.

"I love you more than she does," said Monica.

"See what I mean. Their thoughts are on you all day, every day. I tried everything to dissuade them from putting you before their studies, but they refuse to listen. I thought you might have a solution to the problem."

"Fair dinkum?"

"I want to marry you, Blue," said Natty.

"Huh!" he grunted as his face screwed, and his eyes said it all.

"Will you marry me, Blue?" asked Monica.

"Woo, struth! You're going too fast for me! I'm flattered, but this is something that's new to me," he said as he screwed his face trying to fathom what Natty and Monica were saying.

"Do you love me, Blue?" asked Natty.

"Do you love me, Blue?" asked Monica.

"Yeah, of course I do. I love you both, and I love your sisters, too. I can tell you that love's not on my mind right now, but obviously, it's found me.

"Natty, are you sure you haven't just got a temporary crush on me?"

"Yes, I might be young, but I know about love. My friends in Russia marry for power and prestige but soon became unhappy. I want someone who loves me. I love you for who you are and not for your looks, your title, or your ability."

"Natasha, can I speak to you alone for a minute?"

"Please wait outside until you're called, girls."

"Natasha, what do I tell Natty? I don't want to break her heart."

"Nikolai and I had a somewhat extreme altercation about my attitude towards our children before your ship came in, and your men might've told you that the shouting was so loud that the birds took off from the trees and started the dogs barking. Since then, I've understood how fake I'd been, so now, my advice to you is to just be honest with them, even if it hurts or not."

"Oh, that will break her heart! Well, call them in." When they entered, Blue said, "Girls! Your life is controlled by your parents until you reach the age of eighteen, and after that, you can do whatever you want to do. You must accept what your parents tell you.

"It'd make me happy if you girls were to behave yourselves, and maybe, pray for a solution. You do trust in God, don't you? Is that fair enough?"

Natty and Monica looked at Blue, and nobody said anything for a while.

"Yeah, okay, Blue," said Natty.

"Yeah, of course, Blue," said Monica.

Natasha shook her head and said, "I've got eleven of them."

"This has taken me by surprise, Natasha. Monica and Natty are very lovely girls, and I didn't mean to be the cause of so much trouble."

"Well, we knew it'd happen sometime, but we didn't expect it to be this quick."

Blue got on his horse and rode to his retreat on the riverbank to have a good think. The grassy retreat relaxed him, and solutions to his problems came quick when he gazed at the water.

"Natty?" he said to himself. He spent the rest of the day fishing and thinking about it.

Natty had her own thinking spot, and when she got there, she sat on the grass of the riverbank with her knees up and her arms wrapped around them as a support for her chin. She closed her eyes and prayed.

Twenty minutes later, she was about to get up to leave. "Oh, sorry, I hope I didn't disturb you, did I?"

"Hey?" Surprised, she turned quickly.

"Hi, I'm Gordon. I live over there. Blue said I could take a shortcut home through here and go fishing whenever I want."

"Oh, hi, Gordon."

"I've seen you at school, but I don't talk to people, much. I'm shy."

"Oh, well, don't be shy with me, Gordon. I need some company right now."

He nodded and said, "I've got a spare hand line. Do you want to do some fishing?"

"Yeah, sure, have you got a girlfriend?"

"No, never had one."

"Oh?"

Natty sat next to him on the riverbank and studied him as he talked to her. His concentration was on the fishing line in the river.

They spent an hour talking to each other and discovered that they had similar interests.

It was approaching lunch time when Gordon said, "I better go now. Mum and dad might think that something's happened to me. Can I talk to you at school?"

"Yes, I'd love that," she said and gave him a big smile which he returned.

"We might catch a fish next time. I'll bring some worms."

"Okay."

"See ya."

"Bye," she said and hoped that he would turn and wave to her after walking off.

He walked off and turned. "Bye," he said and waved.

A feeling of love enveloped her.

When she got home, Blue knew straight away that she had just met someone. He said, "Whoever he is, I think you should see more of him."

"Hey?" she uttered, bringing herself out of her daydream.

"You look very pleased with yourself," said Blue.

"Oh, yeah, I just met Gordon."

"Gordon? Oh, yeah! He's a good lad, and I'm going to ask him to work for me in his spare time after school and weekends."

"Yeah?" Her slight look of surprise was replaced with a slow head nod and a slight smile.

Blue could see that she was happy to know that and that a miracle had just taken place.

When Natty walked off, Blue went straight to Monica and said, "Natty's got a boyfriend." He filled her in about the matter.

Monica said, "Wow! That was a quick answered prayer. We all prayed for a solution."

"I don't pray, but now I'm a believer."

Monica told her parents about Natty having a boyfriend, hoping for a change of heart from them, and that they would allow her to propose marriage to Blue because she was only two years away from being an adult. She asked them, "Can I ask him to marry me, please?" She expected them to say no, as usual.

"Will you promise to behave yourself and do what you're told? And you will do your homework, won't you?"

"Huh?" Her jaw dropped, and she went numb with surprise. She had been disappointed for so long about that, and her mother was the only one against it. "You mean you'll allow me to propose marriage to Blue? Right now, and not when I'm eighteen?"

Her mother looked at Nikolai. He gave his head a slight twist and raised his eyebrows. She said, "Well, you've got every intention of asking him when you're an adult, anyway, haven't you?"

"Yes."

"Well, this way I won't have to put up with all your winging and complaining. And of course, some work might get done around here, won't it?"

"Huh! Oh, of course." She looked at her father, and going by his smile, she knew that half the battle was won.

She only had one thing on her mind. She thought, "I've got to find Blue. Oh, wow! Will I ask him now, or will I wait till we're together in a nicer place, like at the creek? No, I can't wait."

She ran to the stables where she knew Ted would be, and said, "Ted, where's Blue?"

"At the river where we go fishing. Going by the looks of it, I better saddle you a horse."

"Thanks." She only had a couple of fingernails left to chew on, but she knew he wanted to know what was going on, and said, "Mum and dad said I could propose marriage to Blue."

"Fair dinkum? The barney your folks had must've had something to do with their change of heart."

"Yeah, sis told me about that.

"Will he marry me, Ted?" She studied him anxiously.

He stopped tightening the saddle and said, "I do the work of two men now because he doesn't know what he's doing anymore."

A bigger smile from the heavens was slapped on her face in an instant.

"There you go. Don't wear him out?"

"Who, Blue?"

"Ha, no, the horse."

She gave a glance without losing her smile before mounting and riding off.

When she got to the creek, he grabbed the reins as she dismounted.

Going by her smile, he knew that she was the bearer of good news of some kind and was anxious to find out what was going on.

She was unsure just how she should go about asking him, and she did not know if he would accept, but she knew she would have to ask sooner or later. She took a deep breath as he gazed at her intently and blurted it out. She said, "Will you marry me?"

He was in a state of shock, and it appeared that her hopes could be dashed. Her heart pounding with anticipation when he gave her the biggest smile she had ever seen on his face. He said, "You mean, your parents agreed to this?"

"They said I could ask you. I spoke with them about it a little while ago."

"Oh," he said.

She was starting to feel a bit sick when he didn't answer straight away, but then he said, "No, I'm afraid that's out of the question. I can't marry you."

"Huh?" she queried as her heart sank to the lowest depths.

"Not now," he said with a smile. "You'll have to wait till you're eighteen."

"Does that mean you will?"

"Yes."

She almost collapsed with relief before she gave a big smile. She threw her arms around him and kissed him on his cheek and said, "Don't scare me like that!"

They sat on a log and discussed the possibilities of either one of them having second thoughts later when age can influence a situation. Both were satisfied and understood exactly what they were getting themselves into.

"I'm more than likely going to lose the friendship of some friends and family, but I really don't care what they think if we don't have their support."

"I feel the same way about it, too."

Fifteen

Action in the outback

Blue remembered that he had arranged a trip to the desert for the blokes a while ago. He said to Ted, "Do you want to go on the trip, mate?"

"You're forgetting I'm off in three days for a month, mate."

"Oh, that's right. With everything going on, no wonder.

"All the info's on my desk. You know where the caves are?"

"Yes, boss! The old caves on the Spinifex track near Camooweal in the northwest of our beautiful state of Queensland. I can remember being told a few times, mate," he said as he shook his head.

"Oh, good. Make sure you give Bob this map when he replaces you."

"Okay." He shook his head again.

"Macca! Go and get Charlie for me."

Five minutes later, Charlie came and asked, "Yeah, boss?"

"I want you to do something that's important. Could you please remind Ted to give Bob the information for the trip? We plan to head off on the day before Bob starts."

"Oh! Has he been on the grog again?" he asked with a smirk on his face as he turned to Ted.

Ted shook his head and said, "He doesn't know what he's doing, mate, he and Monica are getting married."

"Blimey! Yeah? That explains it."

"Explains what?" asked Blue.

"Well, boss, we never forget! You know that."

"Huh?"

"Your mind has gone AWOL, and I'd say it won't be back for a while."

"Oh, yeah, I'll reprimand it later. It'll probably end up dixie-bashing for a few days in the shearer's mess."

"Why the shearer's mess?" asked Ted.

"Because it will have forgotten to go to the drover's mess!"

The blokes had a chuckle to themselves.

"Congratulations, mate. Have the rest of the day off and don't worry about anything. Just give us the key to the beer fridge now before you forget where you put it," said Charlie.

"Yeah, I'm a mess. Sorry."

"No probs, mate."

"She'll be a bit cool at night," said Charlie.

"Yeah, mate, I know. That's the only time we can squeeze it in. They're really looking forward to this trip."

"Okay, I'll organise a barrel of veggies and Bully beef for five. I'll get the boys to put extra fuel and water in Betsy, seeing that you'll be driving on mostly sandy tracks."

"So, Fred fixed the four-wheel drive?"

"Yeah, mate."

"Just Alexander, Grandpa, George, Fred, and yourself going?"

"Yeah, Charlie. Nikolai can't come."

"Plenty of spirits and beer?"

"Nahhhh," he said with a smile-wide smirk on his face.

The men left before sunrise and headed for the desert, west of Mt. Isa.

"And how far are the caves from here, Blue?" asked Alexander.

"Eight hundred and forty miles, mate. We'll be doing a bit of camping, I reckon."

"It sure is hot and dry. There's a lot of wildlife around here, too," said George.

"she can get warm."

It was the first time the family had ever been camping. "Wow, now I understand why you told us to bring our coats. The nights are freezing!" said George.

Fred said, "It's the low humidity. Dry air doesn't hold that much heat."

"Heavens, sitting around the fire like this reminds me of home. But it's the desert and not the snow."

The next morning. "Bacon and eggs for brekky!" hollered Fred as he scraped the huge hotplate after dishing it out.

"Oh, yeah, that smells great! It's not even daylight yet" said George. No one was in any great hurry to get up.

Fred said, "The billy's boiled."

"Did you see that!" shouted Alexander as a big red kangaroo hopped past the truck.

"You wouldn't be sleeping there if you knew what was crawling around at night," said Fred.

Leaning on his elbow in his swag, Grandpa looked in and around it and said, "If anything eats me, it'd probably die from alcohol poisoning.

"Did you hear the pots and pans rattling last night?"

Fred said, "Goannas, mate. They're scavengers."

They admired the surrounding countryside as they enjoyed breakfast.

A piece of canvas had to be put in place to protect whoever was driving from severe sun burn when they headed off.

"Hang on!" A red kangaroo hopped across the track in front of them.

Finally, Camooweal was in sight after days of bouncing around in the sticky and dusty conditions. After looking around the small town for a couple of hours, Blue suggested having lunch at the lake area. "Oh, what a beautiful place. I don't know about you, but I'm going for a swim," said Alexander.

Everyone had fun and decided to stay for a few days. The caves, which date back five hundred million years, could wait a little while longer for them.

Two days of exploring the caves, roughly nine and a half miles southeast of Camooweal, was an adventure the family enjoyed much more than any they had been on in their country of origin.

Everyone wanted to stay longer, but life had to go on at the station.

George spotted a bush track on the map that led to an abandoned mine fifty miles further south on their way home. He said, "Blue, can we go and see the mine not far from here?"

"We'll have to go to town to notify the appropriate authorities, first." Blue pulled up a little distance from the track.

"Why is that?" asked George.

"Mate, no one will know where we are if we don't get home!"

"Look at it, it's straight and flat! What could go wrong?"

Fred looked at George, smiled, and shook his head.

"It's against my better judgement."

"We've never seen an old mine."

"I shouldn't be doing this, mate, but I'll go there to have lunch, okay?" He shook his head.

"Thanks, Blue."

They discovered that the track was fenced off. There was no one around, so they got their shovels out to gain entry and reassembled the barricade after driving through.

Blue studied the surface and the surrounding area before deciding to negotiate the red gravel dirt track with bulldust and corrugation. He adjusted his speed to the conditions knowing that there would more than likely be a dangerous hidden hazard somewhere. He said, "See that? That's bulldust."

Grandpa asked, "What's bulldust? Is it something like bull…?"

"No, Dad!" said Alexander, quickly cutting him off.

"What?" Grandpa was a bit deaf.

"Nothing!" shouted Alexander.

"Well, mate, in dry places like this where there's lots of rain, the dirt breaks down to a fine powder, and when the track isn't used for a while, it's hard to tell where the pits are," said Fred.

"Pits?" queried Grandpa.

"The potholes get big when they take a hiding over time. Big, deep, and dry holes. And when it rains, the fine stuff is washed into them. And when dried, you can work it out for yourself. Yes, deep holes filled with fine dust. They could have deep sharp edges, too, mate," said Fred.

Blue reduced his speed. "It'd be a good idea to expect the unexpected."

The conditions changed forty-five miles down the track, and Blue put his foot down on the accelerator with the much firmer track to drive on without corrugation.

A troop of kangaroos in the distance distracted him for a second, and he failed to observe the change in conditions ahead. "Hold on!"

No one could see anything as the truck skidded to slow down.

Fred shouted, "Bulldust! Brace!"

The truck plunged into a deep pit of the super-fine dust before it could slow down.

A huge cloud of choking powder exploded upwards and outward by the windshield and the front end of the truck, completely engulfing it. The men looked at the windshield that suddenly turned red as the dust blew in through open windows and air vents.

There was a bang and a jolt before the vehicle became airborne and the front end slammed into the track.

The Russian family underestimated the potential for danger to their wellbeing and failed to brace like the experienced blokes. They became missiles and crashed into those in the front.

The dust trailed from the truck as it came to a stop

many yards away.

Shocked, but alive, a couple of the blokes pushed themselves off the others. Grandpa pulled himself upright off the floor with a big smile on his face and said, "Yeah! Let's do that again!"

"Everyone ok?" asserted Blue as he rubbed his ankle.

Fred said, "Our bush-bashing adventures are worse than that, mate," looking at George.

When everyone confirmed that there were no broken bones suffered, they clambered out and made their way to the trackside where they sat rubbing muscles.

Grandpa said, "I'm happy now that I've had my fix."

"Are you okay, boss?"

"Yeah, mate, just a sore ankle."

Shortly, Fred screamed, "The only barrel with water in it is busted. Everyone come and give me a hand to salvage the water that spilt out into the truck, please?"

Everyone ran or limped over to the truck and searched for anything that could be used to scoop or hold water.

Not much in the back of the truck escaped damaged except the recovery equipment box and its contents.

An hour later, every bit of water was stored safely in suitable containers.

Fred checked the truck. "Boss! The driver's side front leaf spring is stuffed. A few other things, too. Day and a half or so to fix.

"I had a feeling to chuck a leaf spring in. We'd be

having a good hike back if I didn't."

"Ok, good work. When you're ready."

"It looks alright under the bonnet. Get yourself on the accelerator while I crank it."

The motor turned over on the third hard turn of the crank handle, and Blue babied the accelerator through the splutters to make the motor purr like a kitten.

Blue said, "We'll have to ration the water because we lost a lot. Fred will be sweating a lot more than us, so he should get a bit more for that. Everyone agree?"

"Of course! You'll fix it, won't you?" asked Alexander.

"Yeah, not a problem."

"Right, water! How do we get water?" asked Blue.

"Ok, go and look for it?" said George.

Grandpa said, "Do a rain dance?" being smart.

"No, we produce it."

"Huh?" queried George.

"We all go and bag the bushes. It's called a water extraction system."

Everyone just looked at him and said nothing as they followed him to the back of the truck. He gathered all the rubberised wet-weather capes and a knife and some string. "Here, grab these and follow me."

He went to a shrub with blue-green foliage in the dense vegetation covering the red sandy dirt and bunched together several of its branches. He bound them together and said, "George, get the cape under the leaves at the bottom of these branches and fold it up to bag them. With both hands, scrunch the cape together at the top and get someone to tie the scrunched cape to the branches with string. Weigh the branches down with rocks to keep them bent over so the condensation from transpiration can run down to the bottom of the bagged section inside."

"Yeah! Transpiration?" queried Alexander.

"Yeah, we sweat the leaves. It gets hot in there, mate. This heat will sweat anything."

Grandpa said, "You wouldn't get much from that, would you?"

"Yeah, quite a bit, mate. A couple of pints a day. We'll survive, anyway."

"Wouldn't it taste funny?"

"Well, you'll probably want to put some vodka in it."

"Ohhhhh."

"You blokes do the same with the rest of the capes, please?" asked Blue.

"I'll have to work on the truck where it is, boss."

"Okay. When George is free, you can use him.

"When you blokes finish bagging the bushes, dig a few holes, four foot in diameter and two foot deep."

"Lord! Are the Germans coming? Just being smart."

"Ha-ha! Water extraction pits, mate. Same as the bags, but we throw the branches in, stick a billy on them, cover it with a cape, and plonk a stone on top in the middle of the cape. The water vapour runs down the inside of the cape to the point where it drips into the billy."

"Heck, are you sure we can get enough to live on?"

"Yeah, plenty of canvas here, mate."

Blue said, "Well, a dozen done and just on dusk. Well done."

"Working on the truck tonight, Fred?" George asked as he helped him fill the kerosene lanterns.

"Yeah, mate.

"Ah, this place gives me the jitters. The bush is a tinderbox, and if the wind keeps up, it could fuel a fire.

"Block the wind while I light the wick, George.

"Should have the old girl finished by lunch tomorrow if I get a bit of sleep, Blue."

"Good, mate, don't wear yourself out."

Just before sundown, the men did the rounds to check the level of water in the extraction systems. There was enough to keep everyone alive.

Grandpa said, "This is much better, a good stiff cool breeze."

Fred said, "I don't like any breeze in these conditions, mate.

"Sleep anywhere but on the track, you could get run over or something."

"Oh, I'm moving, too," said Alexander.

No one slept near the truck.

"Wake me at first light, boss."

"Yeah, sure, mate."

The fauna woke everyone early, and a banging noise

turned their attention to the truck.

"Heck, he got an early start!"

Blue crawled out of his swag and went to the truck. "I'll give you a hand, mate."

"You had an early start," said Grandpa.

"We don't want to be caught with our pants down in a place like this, mate."

"Oh, yeah, the fire thing?" queried Alexander.

"Not only that, mate."

He looked intently at Fred.

On his back, while tightening a nut at the front of the truck, he said, "Rain."

"Wouldn't we be glad to see that?" asked Grandpa.

"Be trapped here, mate. It hasn't been much of a wet season, but we've had cyclones around late March. They turn into rain depressions when they hit the coast."

Grandpa was waiting for him to finish what he was saying.

As Fred was getting up, he said, "Really wet clay is really wet trouble."

The men went around and gathered the bush water. They gave Fred his ration and offered their assistance.

"Is that a storm over there?" asked George.

Everyone turned to look.

Grandpa said, "It looks like it's coming our way."

"That's more trouble than anything," said Fred.

They looked intently at him.

"Dry thunderstorm. Plenty of thunder and lightning

but no rain. It evaporates before it hits the ground. See the rain falling under the grey clouds? It's not hitting the ground, but the lightning still hits the ground, though. That means fire because the bush is dry when it's struck."

"Ew, there's plenty of lightning, too," said Alexander.

Fred stopped looking and got back to work.

The storm was passing over the party, and everyone took shelter from the lightning strikes under the truck.

"Do you think it will cause a fire, Blue?" asked George.

"There's no smoke where it came from. Just hope it stays that way, mate."

"George, hand me that pinch bar?"

"Anything we can do, Fred?" asked Grandpa.

"Yeah, mate, start packing the truck and collect the water."

"Right."

"Watching for smoke, Blue?" asked Grandpa as he carried a box to the truck.

"Yeah, mate, don't trust it." He dropped dirt to see the direction and the strength of the wind.

"Oh, no, is that smoke in the distance?" asked Alexander.

"I'll get my binoculars."

"We may have to leave in a hurry, Fred, how is the truck coming along?"

"Almost done, but I can't rush it."

"Could be smoke. Here, Alexander, see if you can

make it out."

Fred said, "George, jack the truck up another four inches and get me some grease."

When George was looking for grease, Fred tightened a nut with vigour which made the truck sway. He was under the front end with the wheels off when the jack moved and was ejected by the weight of the truck. There was a loud crash which made everyone look around.

"Fred! Are you okay? Fred! Fred!" screamed Blue.

"Yeah, mate, no problem! Keep your shirt on! The truck just fell onto the support stands, that's all."

Since his cousin was killed when his truck rolled backwards off its jack and crushed him to death while he was working underneath it, Fred has always chocked all wheels on the ground and used support stands religiously. The support stands Fred used under the truck were chocks of wood placed on top of spare wheels which lay flat on the ground each side of the front end under the chassis.

"Mate, don't scare me like that!"

"I promise I won't kark it on you. I asked Vera to pray for us before we left.

"George, set that jack up for me, please…"

"Lord, I think it's smoke!"

Blue threw some dirt.

"George, I need you here. Don't worry about that!"

Blue said, "Ok, we're on a track heading west, the smoke is in the south west, there's hot south westerly winds fanning what looks like a wildfire in our direction, and we definitely won't get the truck fixed before the front reaches us. What do we do?"

Grandpa and Alexander, who were standing near George and Fred, studied him, curious to see if he had the answers.

"You tell me, Blue," said Alexander.

"Well, we starve it before it gets here. It looks like the spotting is making it move quicker…"

"Spotting? And how do we starve it?" queried Grandpa.

"Live embers are blown miles ahead of the front starting fresh fires. We fight it! No time to lose. Get your guns!"

"Guns?" queried Grandpa.

"Yeah, we're going to fight fire with fire. Come on!"

The men were bewildered as they followed Blue and got their guns. Blue said, "Alexander, hurry up the track about thirty feet and shoot the grass. Grandpa, you stay here and shoot at the grass while I go down the track. Put the barrel on the grass and shoot."

"That's sure to start a fire!" said Alexander.

"Yeah, mate, we fight fire with fire. The backburn will burn the ground fuel slowly away from us toward the main front with less intensity than the wildfire, but when the front reaches the burnt area, it'll have stopped dead in its tracks. No more ground fuel to burn. Then it'll stop."

"Are you sure this is going to work, Blue? Those flames look to be thirty-foot high," asked Grandpa.

The men started the backburn.

"Come on, come on, burn! Stone the crows!"

"Our backburn is very slow," said Grandpa.

"Yeah, we should've gone twenty foot off the track and started the burn, mate."

"George, concentrate on this! Vera's praying for us, so don't worry about getting roasted."

"Lord, give us a miracle!"

"There should be enough burnt ground, now, mate. Quick, grab that canvas and go to Fred and George!

"Bloody hell! Give us a bit more canvas and get behind the boxes!" said Blue.

"Ahhhh, my trousers are on fire!" screamed Grandpa and frantically whacked at it. "So, this is how I'm going?"

"Whose hair can I smell burning?" shouted Alexander.

"It's yours, mate!"

"Shit!" he screamed as he frantically whacked his head.

"I think this is it!" said Grandpa.

"No, Dad! Don't say that!"

"It's not so hot, now!" shouted George.

Blue stuck his hand up from behind cover to see how hot it was. "Phew! You're right, mate."

"Look out, the canvas is on fire!" shouted Grandpa.

"Ah!" He threw it on the ground.

"We're safe now, but the backburn could've been quicker!" said Blue.

"If we didn't do it when we did, we'd be roasted," said Grandpa.

"Ah, give us some water," said Fred.

Everyone rested behind shelter and drank bush water.

"What else could possibly go wrong," asked Grandpa.

"Ah, sorry for putting everyone through this," said George.

No one said anything, they just slowly got to their feet and threw everything in the back of the truck before Fred said, "Can you drive, boss?"

"Yeah, my ankle is a lot better."

They finally drove off after Fred gave the truck a final check.

"Next time you want to go somewhere, George, we'll drop you off and take off without you," said Grandpa.

"How far to the main road?" asked Alexander.

"About half an hour, mate."

"There's the hill you wanted me to remind you of, boss."

Blue looked at the Zuckschwerdts. "To get through that stuff, I have to put the foot down."

"You better stop and make sure there's nothing on the other side, boss!"

"There won't be anything coming, the track's closed off! Remember? We had to dig the gate post up.

"I've got a bad feeling about this, mate!"

"Ah, bloody hell, mate, she'll be right! What could be there? Maybe an animal. I just want to get the hell out of here."

He hit the bulldust just before the crest at speed. It slowed the truck considerably but not enough to stop it from going airborne behind a huge cloud of red dust it forced out, obstructing their vision.

"Hang on! I can't see a bloody thing!" said Blue.

"Struth!" shouted Fred. The truck cleared the crest and was coming down on top of an aborigine who was crossing the road.

"Did you hear anything? I bloody well didn't see anything," said Blue.

The old man was too slow to react and was driven into the track by the front end of the truck.

Blue slammed on the brakes and skidded to a stop after it bounced a few times.

"Oh, shit!" said Blue as he got out and saw the old man in a mangled heap in the red dust.

"Lord!"

George just looked at the old man and said nothing.

"I told you, mate! The poor bugger," Fred shook his head.

"Big white beard. A spear and a boomerang, his only possessions. He looks a little older than me. Well, at least it was quick," said Grandpa.

"It would've been quick, his head is caved in," said

George.

"Poor bugger was probably going deaf," said Fred.

"What do we do now?" asked George.

"Bury him, I suppose, I don't know. The boss can decide."

"Fred! Fair dinkum, mate. Ah, stone the flaming crows!" He took his hat off and sat on the red sand off the track scratching his head.

"I wonder where his mob is?" asked Grandpa.

"Who knows, they could be miles away," said Fred.

Blue said, "We'll bury him here and go to town to report it."

"Why can't we take him to the hospital in town?" asked Grandpa.

"They'll just tell me to take him out of town and bury him, anyway," said Blue.

"Heck, really!"

"It's an ongoing thing they've got with these people, mate."

They searched the area for any signs of his mob, but no trace was found.

The man was buried and was given some words of sympathy from Grandpa.

When in town, Blue told the blokes to wait in the pub while he reported the event to the police. He went inside the police station and made conversation with the constable, but there was no reporting done.

He went to the pub and sat at the bar with the blokes

when he left the police station. Fred said, "How'd you go, mate?"

"Yeah, mate, they said they'd fix everything up. Just an accident and no need for any witness statements just yet. He said we can do that when we get home. Give them to me and I'll take them in."

"Fair dinkum, mate?"

The Zuckschwerdts studied Blue and were thinking hard but saying nothing, as their intuition picked up on an inconsistency in his mannerism.

"Come on, let's get out of here!" said Blue.

After filling the petrol and water tanks, they were on their way home. Nobody said a word, they just watched the road.

Blue had just deceived himself in the big-time league. He was in no hurry to right the wrong, and there was the danger of not resolving the issue.

The temperature had dropped dramatically, and when they found a good spot on the Diamantina River to rest, they cast their hand lines to try to catch some fish for dinner and calm themselves a little. They caught some silver tandans and spangled perch and decided to set up camp for two days.

They sat around the campfire waiting for the fish to cook and talked about the tragedy.

Alexander said, "I've seen a lot of death and destruction in my time, but that was in time of war. Killing someone then was not a problem for me at all but this is different.

"I suppose now is a good time to get it off my chest. Before the dry law, when everyone was drunk, I was driving home after a wild night out and dead drunk as usual. I was going too fast and lost control of the car going around a corner.

"I had no idea what I hit, but later I found out that the poor soul I ran over was killed, and he was an old man, too. He was probably on his last legs, anyway, but what little life he had left, I took it from him through my stupidity. So, I know exactly how you feel, Blue."

He knew that Blue did a stupid thing, but he also knew that his comment would cut right to the heart of the matter and would make no apology for it. He went on to say, "It's been haunting me for so long, and it feels like I've aged ten years since." He hoped Blue was listening, anyway.

"Heck, Dad! I wondered why you gave up drinking. And, yeah, you started going to church with us. Was that the reason?"

"Yeah George! I lacked the guts to track down his folks to give them the financial support they needed until six months after I found God. Lord, finding you was the best thing that's ever happened to me.

"Since I decided to take responsibility for my actions, I've been at peace." Alexander chose those words deliberately, and he intended giving him all the support he could possibly give, for he considered Blue to be family.

He knew exactly what it was like to be disowned by family in time when support was needed.

Blue sat looking into the fire and said nothing all night.

Everyone sat and mulled over Alexander's words until they realised that the fish was burning.

The monsoons were bringing rain to the north, so the men left the river before the weather worsened.

They were greeted by all when they got back to the station, and Nikolai said, "Next time you go, I'm coming with you!"

Blue grabbed some bully beef and a billy and said, "I'm going to my thinking spot for a couple of days."

Monica knew that there was something wrong when she was ignored. She was about to chase after him when Alexander stopped her. After explaining what had happened on the trip, she said, "How awful, I must go to him."

"No, girl! He'll have to work this out for himself. He needs time alone to think."

"We were just told what happened," said Vera as she approached them.

"Well, all we can do for him now is pray," said Alexander.

Everyone except Grandpa prayed that Blue takes the right decisions and to give healing to all involved in the event.

Monica waited for his return, constantly watching

the track to the river.

When Blue finally turned up, he asked for the witness statements and prepared for a trip, then said, "I'll be gone for a couple of weeks." He waited for the witness statements and gave Monica a smile before getting into his car and driving off.

When he entered the same police station he went to before to report the event, he saw the same constable who asked, "How can I help you, mate?"

"Last week, just out of town, I drove over a hill and hit and killed an old aborigine man on the track, mate. It was my fault because I stopped my mate from checking for traffic on the other side. I drove blindly over it. I just came to report it."

"Did you drag him off the track?"

"Yeah, we buried him."

"Don't worry about it, then."

"Huh?"

"She's right, don't worry about it!"

Blue just stared at the constable, not believing what he was hearing, but he had a good idea what to expect, anyway.

"Mate, they're the sentiments of the town, so there's nothing I can do about it.

"I'll get the boot if I follow this up. It's considered a waste of time, besides, they're just a bloody nuisance, anyway."

"Okay, then," he said and nodded before leaving.

Searching for the aborigine's mob was now his priority, and he spent the next few days asking questions of the locals for any information about it.

His futile attempts to produce results frustrated him but not enough to stop him. He was determined to find the man's relatives no matter how long it took, for a life-changing experience had blown his mind out of the cesspool in which it was dwelling after leaving the police station the first time. The face of a battle-hardened entity slowly appeared out of the darkness of the corridors of his inner vision when he was resting with his eyes closed.

He knew that the entity was friendly, and through telepathy, he knew exactly what was being communicated to him.

Still facing Blue, the entity slowly withdrew into the darkness after the message was given, and he knew that it was confirmation of a higher power wanting to help him.

After four days of searching, he found an old aboriginal woman who told him where he could locate a tribe.

The next day, he drove into the unmanaged aboriginal reserve and spoke to a middle-aged man. "Are you missing an old fella?"

"Ah, old Charlie, him not see two weeks. You know about him?"

"Yeah, mate, I'm afraid so."

"You sound like not real good thing happen to

Charlie?"

"He was on the track, and I ran over and killed him. I should've checked the other side of the hill before driving over it."

"Ah, poor fella, him do that all the time, no listen, sometime sleep on track. Nothing we could do. Charlie, him own boss and did what him wanted. We expected it."

"Where's his family?"

"Come".

After explaining everything again, the old man's daughter, Yindi, gave him a big hug and said, "You good white fella, him rest now with Ancestors in The Dream Time, incredibly happy now. Him bad sick and ready to die, and he suffer much. That's why I know him happy now.

"The government came and took my two kids. Awfully bad. Not see them again." She broke down and cried. "Me happy that dad is happy, but everyone's sad that kids were taken."

"Have you got a photograph of your children?"

"One only. All I got."

"Can I have this to show my friend in the government?"

"You help try find?"

"I'll do everything I possibly can to find them."

Blue wrote down all the information needed to conduct a thorough search.

"You family now, ok?"

"Ok." He told her where his grave was and joined the family for the afternoon.

The woman told him that old Charlie was very spiritual and that he was wanting to cross over to be with loved ones he communicated with regularly through the 'bones' divination oracle.

Four hours later, he left the reserve and went to the pub in town. The next day he headed for home with a hangover and a whole new perspective on life.

Everyone came racing out when the dogs announced his arrival. He was somewhat worse for wear when he went inside where he explained everything to everyone. "Will you all forgive me? I was guilty of being influenced by immoral particularistic sentiments that white fella has for the black fella. Had it not been for Alexander's influence in the matter, I'd still be in the dark…"

"The government forcibly removed her children?" queried Alexander.

"Yeah, mate. Some nincompoops with clout in policy making in the government have worked their magic. They've got everyone believing that the blacks have a bad colour. They think that, by assimilating them with whites, they'll rid the country of an unhealthy condition…"

"What!" strongly asserted Vera.

"Yeah, well, Yindi is very distressed as are many families.

"My local member of parliament is a friend of mine. I'll get him to track down her kids for me."

That afternoon, Blue went to town and spoke to Bob about his endeavour. He told Blue that he knew about the removal of children in that area and would investigate the matter for him.

The next day, Bob rang and said, "Good news, mate. We've found the kids, and you can adopt them, too."

"Oh, fantastic, mate!"

Blue drove to Mt. Isa to sign the adoption papers and take possession of two beautiful, brainwashed, and depressed children who, once out of that place, were extremely happy to be on their way to be reunited with their family again.

Yindi had no idea that her life was about to be transformed forever. Happiness and love replaced despair as Blue drove through the reserve to her desert shack, and when the children saw their mother, they screamed with joy. With shock written on her face, she came running with open arms to greet them. "Charlie came to me in dream. Him tell me he will look after me, soon. Much love soon." She sobbed as she hugged her children.

When Blue got back to the station, he told everyone what happened, and Vera said, "Running over old Charlie was a miracle in disguise, so don't go blaming yourself anymore about things you may think are bad. When I was young, I remembered the father at church saying, 'God works in mysterious ways.' So, whatever happens, accept it and think why it happened because everything happens for a reason. I've always found that when something bad happened, I got upset and angry, but later I realised that I was glad it worked out that way. I'm sure we're all being guided, but unfortunately, some of us don't listen and get flustered and take it out on those close to us. I'm talking about my friends in Russia."

Sixteen

Weird miracles

Two days later, a phone call came to the station. Natasha was the only one around. "Hello."

"Hello, I'm Bill, can I please speak to Vera?"

"Hold on a tick." She handed the phone to George who was walking past. "Bill."

"Oh?" He gestured to her as she stood looking. She left the room.

"Yeah, Bill, I'm, ah, Yuri, her cousin. Vera is out for a while."

"I'll be unable to call later, so can you please give her a message for me?"

"Sure."

"Tell her to meet me at Victoria Barracks in Brisbane at noon next Wednesday. If she fails to turn up, I'll understand."

"Will do, Bill."

"Thank you."

He stood looking at the floor thinking for a while before he left.

When Vera got back to the station, George said nothing and tried to avoid her for as long as possible.

When Vera finished unpacking the groceries, she called out to him and persisted until there was no way he could avoid her any longer. She said, "I thought you might've been outside or something."

"Didn't you hear me answer you?"

"No."

"Oh." He thought he had better decide fast. He thought, "Can I live with myself if I were to deceive myself and her? Her mum would probably tell her that Bill rang, anyway."

"Are you okay?"

"Oh, yeah. Ah, I almost forgot. Bill rang."

She stopped what she was doing and turned. "Oh?" She looked at him waiting for some clarification.

He looked at her deep in thought.

"What did he say?"

"He said, 'Tell Vera that I've found another woman,' and he hung up."

"What!"

"No, he didn't say that. But that's how I feel, anyway."

After five seconds, he gave her the message.

"Did he actually say, 'Tell her to meet me'?"

"Yep."

"He could've 'asked' me to meet him."

"Thanks for being honest. You could've ..." She turned to see if her mother was eavesdropping, but he knew what she was saying.

"I'll go and talk with him on Wednesday."

George drove her to Brisbane the following Wednesday and waited in the car outside Victoria Barracks. "I'm so happy to see you again, Vera. I had no idea if my mail had been misdirected or not. Is everything still good with us?"

"We'll see. Do you still want me to go to England with you?"

"But of course. That's where my work is…"

"Would you move to Australia to live with me?"

"You know I can't do that. You'll love it in England."

"Well, Bill, I'll write you a letter soon and let you know."

"I thought we might have lunch or something."

"I have to go; my cousin is waiting for me."

"Oh, okay. You'll love the family when you meet them…"

"Bye."

He stood dumbfounded and watched her walk off.

When she got back to the car, she sat for a while and asked, "George, would you move to America with me?"

"Well, yeah, I'd move to China with you if you wanted."

"Even if you had important work and family elsewhere?"

He knew straight away that Bill wanted her to move to England with him. "Well, yeah! It'd be a selfish act of arrogance if I were to make assertions of that nature. We can work together to get around things like that."

She sat and looked out the window of the car deep in thought. She turned to him and asked, "Do you really mean that?"

"Of course."

"Let's go home."

When they got back to the station, Blue greeted them. He said, "Did you get things sorted out, Vera?"

"I'm pretty sure I did, actually."

Despite a little doubt, George stayed confident. He remembered her asserting trust and faith all the time, so he tried hard to practice it, too. It was all he could do, anyway.

Blue received a telegram from a business associate wanting him to talk business at his station in the Flinders Ranges. He asked the Zuckschwerdts if they were interested in going with him. They accepted and packed their personal stuff and loaded it in the truck with the other supplies that Charlie had arranged that night for the trip.

The drive would have them crossing some of the worst corrugated and dusty roads in the outback which would test the vehicle to the extreme. With roughly thirteen hundred miles of punishment, they had to make regular stops to check for loose nuts and bolts that held the truck together and to have time out for a stretch. The water-filled canvas bag on the front bumper provided cold water in the heat, and they slept in the tents at dusk on each leg of the seven-day drive. On the seventh day, Alexander said, "Those mountains have vivid splash of every colour. The blues, purples, and all the warm colours as well in the foothills are breathtaking, by Jove."

"The Flinders Ranges, mate."

Grandpa said, "That sky is black over the ranges, and the colours stand out against the black sky."

"Yeah, mate. It looks like a bit of rain falling up there."

They were approaching a crossing of a dried riverbed whose banks were lined with huge red gums. George said, "Is that a car in the tree over there?"

"It sure is!" said Alexander.

"There must've been a lot of water to put that up there!" said Grandpa.

"Yeah, mate. A lot of branches and stuff up there, too."

"That'd be twenty foot up in that tree," said George.

"Strange," said Grandpa, "where did so much water come from?"

"Look! Someone up ahead," said George.

"An aborigine on horseback," said Blue.

He slowed when the man waved him down, and when he stopped alongside of the horseman, the man said, "You no cross yet, boss! Spirit strong, tell me."

Blue looked around to see if it was a trap or not. He said, "Why not? Everything looks fine to me. I see no reason why we should wait."

As they spoke, another vehicle pulled up behind Blue's truck. Before the driver got out of his vehicle, the horseman said once again, "No cross yet, boss! Danger!"

"Danger?" queried Blue.

The Zuckschwerdts studied the man's behaviour but said nothing.

The man stopped talking and looked up at the chasm not far away.

As everyone looked in the same direction, they heard a thundering sound that was progressively getting louder. As the driver of the other car approached the men, a huge wall of water exploded out into the dry river crossing.

Everyone was gobsmacked. "Had you not stopped us when you did, we would've been in the middle of that river crossing right now!" said Alexander.

No one said anything, they just watched the churning cascade lift uprooted trees and smash them into the boulders like they were twigs. Alexander said, "Now we know how that car got up there. I wonder what happened to whoever was in it?"

The others said nothing and continued to watch the spectacle for the rest of the day, but they mulled over what he said.

When they went to set up camp in a small clearing off

the road a little further back, they invited the horseman and the other driver to join them for a cuppa. They accepted, and when they sat back with a coffee watching the fire, Blue asked the horseman, "How did you know that was going to happen?"

The driver of the other car asked the man, as he spoke his language. The driver of the other car said to Blue, "He said, 'Where we are here in the sunshine is deceiving because up in the top of the mountains, where the rain falls, the water in the expanse of the catchment comes down through hundreds of gullies and merge in one big river. When the mass of water hits the narrow chasm, the built-up water shoots out the other end pretty fast.' He knows this place like the back of his hand."

Blue said, "Well, mate, you learn something every day."

Nikolai said, "I would've driven right into that."

Blue said, "Ask him if he knows what happened to whoever was driving that car in the tree."

The man asked, and after the aborigine spoke, he said, "He said he stopped a man and a woman, but they ignored him and sped off. Sad, never seen them again.

"I see him on his horse down here all the time trying to warn people when it rains up in the ranges because it's such a big trap."

Everyone stayed until the river was safe to cross, and when it was, Blue and the family drove off, but they were a lot wiser from the experience.

Blue got his business affairs sorted out and they shared the driving on the way back.

When they got back to the station, Blue went straight to the fridge and grabbed beers for himself and the men, and they all sat on the front verandah with the women and girls to discuss the events at the river. Blue said, "I reckon Vera had been praying for us again."

Adelaide said, "You could be just going for a drive or go camping and get killed so easily."

"Yeah, fail to give this beautiful country of ours the respect she deserves, and you could be in big trouble," said Blue.

Business was quiet, so early holiday pay was given, but instead of going to town for holidays, the men stayed at the station. They scrounged around for timber and sheets of iron, and when they had a good supply, they set about digging holes and cutting timber.

Natty and Mary heard the men hard at work building something and went to investigate, and when they saw Nikolai working with the men, they asked him what they were making. He told them that they were building a new doghouse. The girls watched for a while and left.

Blue knew what they were up to but said nothing to the girls.

It only took a few days to knock over with all the blokes on the job.

Blue got the girls to check out the new structure when the blokes were finished. Mary said, "It looks more like a cubby house, Ted, and do the dogs look out that window?"

"Yeah, Mary, they stand up on their hind legs to look out," said Ted, and gave her a smile.

"Oh, you're helping too, Dad?"

"Yeah, why not."

Natty said, "It's pretty big, and do they sleep in those big bunk beds?"

"Blue could answer that for you, Natty."

"Well, Natty, the blokes told me that they, and your dad, wanted to do something special for you girls…"

"What?"

"Yeah, as you can see, there are sufficient bunks for you and all your younger sisters…"

"Ahhhhhhhhhhh!" shouted Natty as she ran to Nikolai and the four blokes, Ted, Cliff, Fred, and Charlie. Mary joined in to give each of them a big hug, about which the blokes were happy.

Ted said, "Your dad and the blokes told me, and I agree, that it was worth it just to see your smiles."

The girls went back for a second round of long hugs.

No one could get them out of it, and they wanted to sleep in it that night. The dogs were just as excited as they were, and seeing that the girls were obliging, they ended up sharing it with them.

The cubby house was built to keep snakes out, so every precaution was taken for their safety.

The girls were so excited about interior decorating

and wasted no time making their beds and putting up curtains. Nikolai even helped paint it.

Everyone stood around chatting and watched them have fun, and eventually, they soaked in the beauty of the bush and its inhabitants, all of which were noisy except for the snakes and goannas.

The dogs were happy in their own beds beside the bunks.

Blue received a phone call after a few days of peace and quiet. "Jacko, here, mate."

"Jacko! Where did you get to?"

"Birdsville. Look mate, can we cut the formalities, something important has come up?"

"Yeah, mate."

"An aboriginal family came across a truck belonging to the son of a friend of mine off the track near Birdsville. I met him here three days ago, and he said he was going to go straight home but obviously went walkabout instead. Could you help in the search?"

"Why didn't he follow his tracks back to the main track?"

"We had a couple of dust storms, and he was nowhere to be found when the family found the truck. They came across it after the second dust storm which covered all tracks, including those of his vehicle. Obviously, he wandered off in the direction he thought would take him back to the track."

"It must've been a howler?"

"Too right, mate."

"Why did he go off the track?"

"His truck was found near an old relic of a truck, maybe he saw it and went to investigate just before the first storm."

"What was he driving?"

"It's the same as yours, but it was bogged down to the diffs."

"Were the tyres deflated?"

"No, he's not experienced."

"Oh, well, the B.E.2. will have a good old workout with this one, then."

"Yeah, it's a good reconnaissance plane, mate."

"She can do with a good run. She's been grounded for a while.

"Is there plenty of fuel at Birdsville?"

"Yeah, everything you need is here, mate."

"Okay, Jacko. We'll be there as soon as possible, mate."

"How'd you like to go to Birdsville, Nikolai? Alexander has a fear of flying. Am I right, mate?"

"Splattering air machines make me nervous!"

"What! Splattering?"

"Where's your sense of adventure, mate?"

"Seeing that you put it that way. Yeah, why not?"

"Good, then we'll get cracking. Every minute counts."

Ted got the car ready and waiting at the front for Blue to drive to his other property five miles away where his plane was housed in a small hanger, and Charlie rang Bill to have it ready to go as soon as they arrived.

When he and Nikolai reached the hanger, the plane's engine was running. A quick introduction was made as their personal gear and equipment was loaded. Blue shouted, "It's noisy, isn't it? But don't worry, mate, It's stable and reliable. The military use them for recon-naissance missions, but the poor payload means that the gear is limited to essentials only, but we'll be com-fortable. Just scream out If there's anything you want to know up there. With the wind and the engine noise, it gets a bit hard to hear."

"Okay," he shouted as Blue was strapping him in. "Canvas and wood? I won't go crashing through it if we hit a bit of turbulences, will I?"

"You'll be okay if you take a bit of your weight off the seat by lifting yourself, but make sure your feet are on the wooden frame and not on the canvas. We don't want to lose you."

Nikolai's quick glance at Blue revealed a face of horror. He had never been flying before, but he thought it was an opportunity to do something different before he became too stagnant in his personal life, but the way he was looking at the plane, he might have had second thoughts about going.

"Don't worry, mate! I'm only joking."

"I think I'll just take your advice, anyway. I don't trust this thing."

Blue taxied the plane to the end of the runway and powered the engine for maximum propeller thrust. The plane bounced a couple of times before it was airborne, which made Nikolai's grip tighten on the frame as his focus turned to every noise and rattle.

After a while, he shouted, "Wo!" as the plane suddenly dropped, making him grip the cockpit with extra bite as he quickly scanned the plane's wings.

"Just turbulence, mate!" screamed Blue from the aft cockpit of the fabric-covered wire-braced fuselage. Blue could see him shaking his head, which put a smile on the character's face.

When Blue touched down at Birdsville airport, he was greeted by Jacko and the local authorities who were waiting for his arrival while aboriginal trackers and other private plane owners searched the area around the missing man's truck. They walked to the command centre which was a shed in the red dirt near the airport tower.

After quick introductions, Blue asked, "Have you found any tracks at all?"

The local policeman, Sid, said, "No, but the truck was turned and facing the main track. After the storm, he probably thought he should walk in a direction out from the back of it, thinking that was the way he drove in. The trackers are searching for tracks out from there."

"Okay, good work, mate. Give me a look at this map.

"Do you know if he had water or blankets?"

"Haven't got a clue, mate," said Sid.

"Ok, I'll search this area before sundown, and this is the information for the tower. I'll get going."

Sid said, "Will do."

He and Nikolai took off to start their search and soon spotted the aboriginal trackers. He decided to do a wider sweep of the area that was marked on his chart, and Nikolai noticed a set of tracks as the sun was disappearing over the horizon. Blue said, "Mark the position on the map, mate. We've got to get back, now."

At the shed, the other searchers were having coffee and sandwiches that some local women had prepared for them. Blue said, "Nikolai found a set of tracks, and the aboriginal trackers were heading straight for them. Right here." He pointed the position on the map. "Now we know where to concentrate our efforts tomorrow. Be cold tonight, too, hey?"

One of the locals said, "Yeah, mate. I wouldn't make it without a coat, at least."

Nikolai could see that no one was making a big deal or complaining about what he considered to be some daft individual whose stupidity was putting them to a lot of trouble. He noticed that everyone was treating the search as being important. In his country, if someone was that stupid, they deserved to suffer the consequences of their actions. He thought of the words Vera spoke about the learning story and having compassion, and he had a good think about learning from one's mistakes. He said, "I suppose you have to learn from your mistakes, hey?"

One local, Bazza, said, "Yeah, mate, in this country, ya can't expect to know everything she's going to throw at ya. You learn or leave this life. We all learn the hard way, and we sympathise with each other because we've been there."

Nikolai said nothing because in his country mistakes are written in books for one to learn from. He thought, "How tough you'd have to be to learn the hard way. I'm still learning at my age, huh!"

Blue and Nikolai stayed at the Birdsville Hotel where the owner gave them free accommodation and meals.

In bed, Nikolai though, "What Vera said about everything happening for a reason. Well, I needed to come on this trip. How it has opened my eyes."

Everyone was up before dawn, and the searchers on the ground were driving through the red sand to the position where the tracks were seen.

Before the search resumed, the searchers who had planes were told by Blue to stand down until further notice, as there was no point in everyone flying around getting in each other's way when there was no need for it.

Blue and Nikolai took off in the plane and soon spotted the aboriginal trackers who spent the night bedded down on their search trail. Blue shouted at Nikolai over the noisy engine and pointed when he spotted the man. He stood waving with both arms as Blue circled. On his way back, he flew low over the men and gave a wing wave by dipping one wing and quickly dipping the other before straightening up to give the signal for them to proceed to the area where the plane circled, which they knew, anyway.

The trackers had proceeded to the area as Blue headed back to the airport to notify every one of the man's successful rescue.

When Blue got back to the shed, the man's parents could not wait to hear what he had to say. He instinctively knew who they were and just said, "Good news! Your son has been found, and he looked to be in good spirits when I flew over."

"Oh, thank God! And you, too."

"Thanks, but all the credit goes to this policeman and the aboriginal trackers. They just showed me the way with their skills."

Blue, the searchers who stayed behind, and the man's parents got to know one another well.

Attitudes were having a major overhaul, and when everyone arrived, confirmation of that happening was apparent, as young Bartholomew swore that, on his next trip, he would religiously adhere to the proven laws of the land, which were organisation, notify authorities, and stay with your vehicle if broken down. His father, Tom, said, "Your ordeal will not only be a lesson to you, but it will serve as an important word-of-mouth tool for good advice for you friends who will hear of it." Nikolai was starting to see how Australia made Australians.

Before Blue taxied his plane on the runway for the flight home, Nikolai conducted his own inspection of the plane to satisfy himself that there were no cracks or torn canvas and made sure that his safety harness was tight and was not going to fail him.

Seventeen

Family in the water with a great white shark

Blue's sister, Louise, was with the zuckschwerdts to greet Blue and Nikolai on their return from the outback. "It's about time!" asserted Blue as he gave her a warm hug.

"I thought It'd be nice if we all spend a couple of days at my place in Pratten before we head off to my holiday home at Burleigh Heads. Everyone's for it, so what about you two?"

"That sounds like a plan, girl." Nikolai was quick to accept, too.

When everyone arrived at Pratten, they followed Louise on a dirt track into the bush for a short distance and pulled up at a log cabin. Louise said, "It's only an acre but big enough for me."

Adelaide said, "This is lovely."

"Thanks. I love watching the birds chase after the goannas that hunt for their eggs in the treetops. All kinds, little ones, big ones, and in between ones join forces to chase them away. The sulphur-crested cockatoos land in front of them and intimidate them by screeching loudly with their wings widespread and a raised crest while the smaller birds move in and perch in the branches of nearby trees awaiting their turn to dive bomb them in flight, one after another, continuously."

"Wow! We'll have to watch out for them," said George.

"Well, the first thing we do around here is have a cuppa. I'll show you around after that."

After Louise showed everyone around the property, the men fired up the outdoor barbecue to get the meat cooking while the women prepared the salad.

In the cabin with the women and girls, Louise said, "Ah, I feel really pleased with myself. Yesterday, this scruffy looking bloke pulled up in his four horse-drawn buckboard and asked me if I'd like a load of firewood for half price.

"I was out of wood and accepted, so he went off and came back in an hour.

"He started unloading it when he came back. I said, 'What's that!' He said, 'Firewood.' I said, 'That's rubbish! It's rotten, and it's not even rotten hardwood! I don't want it, so you can put it all back on your wagon and go.

"I'd always been a weak person and allowed myself

to be exploited by predators and manipulators, but I was at the point where I'd just had enough, so I lashed out without fear of his acting in retaliation, should he be inclined to be that way.

"He was stunned, and he just looked at me with a look of shock.

"He showed his true colours when he suddenly picked his rubbish up and threw it in the back of his wagon with such force that it unsettled the horses and made them turn to see what was going on.

"I just stood and watched him, and when he finished loading, he jumped on the seat and grabbed the whip and started whipping the horses and screaming abuse.

"The horses bolted so fast that he fell back onto the rubbish wood in the back.

"Surely, the horses knew what they were doing. They didn't go back the same way they came from; they went down a small track across a dry creek with a steep incline, but they went so fast through there that the wagon went airborne at the top of it, sending the man and his rubbish firewood airborne and crashing down in a heap.

"Those horses didn't show any sign of wanting to slow down. No doubt they would've been abused a lot by him, too."

Vera said, "Good on you. It feels great to have your power back, doesn't it?"

"Yeah. When the horses bolted, I started laughing

and screaming about how pleased I was with myself, having just stuck up for myself for the first time in my life."

Monica said, "Wow! That was so brave of you."

"Oh, thank you."

Louise said, "Oh, there they go. Can you hear the birds going off their nut?"

"Natasha said, "Oh yeah."

"I've never seen that goanna have a moment's peace."

They went outside and joined the men at the barbecue and watched the birds attack the mischievous predator.

When the goanna went away, Mary said, "You're very pretty, and I love your long blond hair."

Blue said, "I'm so proud of that girl. You know, she refused to marry a millionaire businessman who loved her because she didn't love him.

"He wooed her with expensive jewellery which she wouldn't accept but was forced to keep."

"Thanks, Blue. But there's no point in marrying or being with someone if you don't love them. It'll just destroy you in time.

"You know, Blue's overcome a mountain of a challenge. Did you know that he suffered paraplegia, twice?"

"You've never mentioned this to me in all the time I've known you, Blue," said Alexander.

"Ah, it's nothing, really.

"The reason why it took so long for me to get on

my feet was because I kept exercising my muscles when they were too weak to do anymore. I thought I was going backwards because I was so weak, when all I really needed was to rest them because they were too overworked…"

"Oh, I didn't know paraplegics could walk again," said George.

"Yeah, mate. The spinal cord was just damaged but not severed. Incomplete.

"Anyway, I finally worked it out and started doing it all properly the second time round…"

"Second time?" queried Adelaide.

"Yeah, I got myself walking after ten years, but I didn't stretch my muscles before and after my exercising, mainly when doing my leg weights. My muscles tightened up around the sciatic nerve, and that's when ten years of hard work went down the drain in a flash.

"You see I was in too much of a hurry to get on with life to worry about stretching properly which took so long. I just had a quick stretch and went about doing the things I wanted to do, but when I got going the second time round, I swore that I'd never go through that a third time.

"I disciplined myself to exercise properly but still had a lot to do in my everyday life, so I exercised enough to maintain a level where I didn't go backwards. However, I wasn't going forward, too, so I planned to get serious with it when I was ready.

"When I was, I pushed myself to exercise more but not forgetting to rest the muscles, too.

"It wasn't long before I could see improvement in my strength, so I went for it knowing that I'd be strong enough to walk in no time.

"Frustration was the biggest enemy. Things would fall through my lap, and I'd have a few hairy transfers where I almost ended up on the floor, but somehow, I managed to work it out to overcome the worst of it. But I've always missed the freedom to just go walking on a bush track or swimming at the beach."

"How'd you injure your back in the first place?" asked Vera.

"After celebrating my 40th birthday with a few mates and a good number of longnecks, we decided that we'd have some fun and take the farm wagon for a bit of a spin.

"We were so intoxicated that we couldn't see what we were doing, and when my mate was hitching the team, he didn't do a particularly good job with the straps.

"We thought we'd have a bit of a bash on the washed-out bush track on top of the mountain half a mile away.

"I was in the back of the uncovered wagon with three others and two were up front with the bloke driving the team.

"Although being bounced around a fair bit, the driver thought things could be livened up a bit more, so he gave it to the team by lashing them with the reins and screamed at them in a drunken stupor, which made them bolt with extra pull, breaking something.

"The team broke free from the wagon and bolted, leaving the free-wheeling wagon to find its own way on the rough track which wasn't far from the steep slope of the mountain. It was a long way down, too, but fortunately, there were no trees or big rocks to crash into when the wagon thought it'd take a shortcut home and headed for the slope.

"We managed to stay in the wagon, but most of us were thrown on top of each other when it bounced and crashed as it got going.

"It went airborne when it hit a big bump, throwing us all up and crashing back down with it. I landed on my shoulder as I grabbed hold of the sideboard, and one of the blokes grabbed hold of me and stopped me from falling off.

"The wagon did a good job not to do any violent turns, though, and it slowed down in a large clearing down the bottom with all of us intact but a little worse off for wear and tear.

"I cracked the vertebra at the T 5/6 and 6/7 level when I crashed down on my shoulder, and it took twelve years for the calcification to build up on the injured discs to eventually squash the spinal cord. The body doesn't know when to stop sending calcium to an injured disc, apparently."

"Wow! You really do know how to rough it," said

George.

"Yeah, mate, but why suffer for a long time by doing stupid stuff in the first place?"

The men opted to rough it in the tents. There was nothing that was going to stop the girls from doing the same, so Blue pitched a huge army tent that accommodated everyone.

They sat around the fire telling stories while waiting for the damper to cook, and they enjoyed themselves so much that they were unaware of the time. They had a couple of hours sleep before starting the new day, which was enough.

They woke with the smell of coffee in the air.

No one was in a hurry to get out of bed, and Louise had to encourage them to get up and have breakfast so they could start the day.

At the breakfast table, Louise said, "We've got a big paddock to play cricket in…"

"Yeah!" said Natty, whose approval was echoed by all the girls.

They were denied the right to do what they wanted to do because of the outdated attitudes of their ignorant teachers, tutors, and carers.

They proved themselves to be worthy contenders when they showed the men up on the field. They had so much fun that it ended up being an all-day match.

It was obvious that the girls showed a marked improvement in their will to be creative and demonstrated their enthusiasm clearly.

The full day's activities and fresh air knocked them for a six, and there was no need for anyone to assert their authority on them for being unruly. But, unfortunately, they got to bed early without having their marshmallows over the fire and stick damper.

The day had come for swapping broad-brimmed felt hats and boots for broad-brimmed straw hats, beach towels, and ankle-biting swimming costumes.

They arrived at Burleigh Heads at noon and set up a picnic spot on the grass in the shade of a huge pine tree near the sand.

Blue pumped up some motorbike tyre tubes for the girls to keep them afloat in deep water. The water in which they intended swimming was deep enough for Monica and Mary to stand without a buoyancy device. They could walk out to the sandbar with the men, but the smaller children were supervised by Natasha and Adelaide in shallow water close to shore.

Blue, Nikolai, Vera, Alexander, George, Monica, Mary, and Grandpa waded through the shallow gutter to reach the sandbar and went out a little further where the girls could still stand in waist-deep water.

There were no rips, and the water was calm, so they splashed around and had fun.

After twenty minutes, they were startled by something that leapt out of the water and splashed down in front of them, and before they could do anything, another one appeared as it, too, leapt out of the water and splashed them. The group bunched up into a tight-knit formation. The water churned around them, and it soon became obvious that they were being circled by a pod of dolphins, creating an environment of terror for the girls but one of curiosity for the men and Vera.

Everyone was too distracted and consumed by the spectacle to bother physically protecting the girls, and when Mary saw a gap in the formation, she seized the opportunity to leave the group and try to swim back to shore.

Everyone turned when Monica screamed, "Mary!"

Blue started swimming to reach her after she made a run, but he was stopped by a dolphin that physically blocked his path, and it countered every attempt he made to swim around it with another block. He yelled, "It's stopping me! It won't let me go after Mary."

They knew that the behaviour of the pod was frightening but non-life threatening, but they could not understand why they were acting the way they were.

Their focus of attention was on Mary, and they were able to get a glimpse of her through the formation.

Vera said, "That dolphin is making her come back!"

"What!" shouted Alexander.

"Why are they doing that, Blue?" asked Grandpa.

"I don't know. It's a bit scary, though. I'm actually a little bit worried."

"Here comes Natty!" shouted Vera. "Come here!"

She grabbed the frightened girl.

"I'm okay, sis! It didn't hurt me."

"It's like they don't want us to swim to shore!" said Blue.

Vera wrapped her arms around Natty and prayed. She then said, "It's okay, don't worry. Have no fear."

Everyone heard Vera, but they could also hear some shouting from the shoreline.

Alexander asked, "Can you hear what they're shouting about?"

Their attention was fixed on Natasha and Adelaide shouting and pointing.

"They're pointing over there."

They all looked through and around the pod splashing out of the water to get a better view, and it was a bit easier to see while they were standing in water up to their waist.

There were more dolphins leaping out of the water in the direction where Natasha and Adelaide were pointing. Blue said, "I can see a pretty big fin over there, mate!"

"Is it a shark, Blue?" asked George.

"Hoh! Yeah, mate! He's a big one, too, going by the size of that fin. It looks like they're chasing him out to sea."

Grandpa said, "Yeah, he's taking off with a whole lot of dolphins after him.

"You know, I was terrified before I saw the reason for

all this, Blue."

"Those dolphins were protecting us from that shark?" asked Monica.

"Yeah, they sure were," said Blue.

A gap opened on the shoreline side of the formation, and it appeared that the dolphins were trying to guide them to safety.

The group hastened to shore through the gutter while still under the protection of the pod.

When they reached the safety of the shore, the dolphins joined the rest of the pod to chase the great white shark back out to sea.

No one went near the water for the rest of the day. They dried themselves as they watched the action and discussed what just happened, which Vera called a miracle.

For days after their return to the station, the event dominated all discussions.

On Monica's birthday, she and Blue carried out their wedding plans and attended the church in town for their marriage ceremony and had their reception at the station.

Everyone was involved with the preparation of meals and organising tablets and chairs, of which there were plenty, as the invitation list was long.

Celebrations continued into the early hours of the morning, and the couple was so exhausted that their honeymoon had to wait until they both recovered, which was a week later.

Natty and Gordon were growing fonder of each other, and everyone had a good idea of what to expect from those two.

Grandpa, Alexander, and his family decided on staying at the station, and upon researching business options in the area, they decided on starting up an automobile mechanical repair garage in town.

Grandpa's health took a dive for the worse which landed him in hospital, and when recovering after surgery, he looked to be a changed man that all family members picked up on when they went to visit him. He said, "The strangest thing that I'd ever experienced happened to me when I was under the knife.

"I was looking down on you lot when you were crying, and I was telling you not to worry because I was alright. No one heard me, and then I found myself soaring over a team of wild brumbies that were galloping through the bush. I felt free and at peace, and I really didn't want to come back, but this old man kept telling me things. He said, 'You're not ready for retirement, you've got work to do.' I was a bit reluctant to come back, but here I am."

"Really! An old man? What sort of work have you got to do, Grandpa?" asked George.

"The old man said, and I quote, 'All those times you were spared, and you thought it was just luck, were miracles from divine intervention. You've got a wealth of knowledge we want you to share with the world.' I was about to ask him how, but he answered my question before I even asked it. He said, 'Write a book. Everything you need will be provided, and your family will continue to enjoy the protected and care the way they have been in the past. But it would be good if you showed a bit of gratification and be more positive.'

"You know, I can understand that. My knowledge should help a lot of people."

"I never thought I'd see the day," said Adelaide.

Grandpa had a new lease on life and looked healthier and happier than ever before.

The Australian federal government took control of meat production, distribution, and prices in the state to ensure that a cheap and reliable supply of bully beef (tinned corned beef) was sent to the soldiers abroad, and as Blue's lucrative cattle business became less profitable, consequential to the government's actions, he gave up cattle producing and concentrated his efforts on his horse breeding business.

When he discovered that the mechanical repair business was taking off in leaps and bounds, Blue joined forces with the Zuckschwerdts.

Everyone was telling Vera how much she and her cooking and baking would be missed if she and George decided to move to Brisbane.

Blue's father was getting frail in his old age, so he was moved to the station where he could be better looked after. He and Blue had the time to catch up on missed opportunities in their relationship. His presence was welcomed by Alexander, whose sheer delight was apparent upon learning of his chess skills. Although the mature Australian's declining concentration gave the baron a good edge, he was still having fun doing what he wanted to do.

The way George had been spending more time with his grandpa, suggested that he wanted to get to know him a lot better before he made the ultimate transition. He had seen it so many times in the families of close friends just how easy it was for someone to pass before their loved ones could spend enough time with them to get to know them better.

As time went by, there was a noticeable change in Mary's behaviour toward Macca, and she had her eyes firmly set on him. He returned her smiles, but he dared not go further, and she could see that she would have to be the one to make the first move to break the ice and spent days thinking of ways to get a first date.

He would decline offers to go to town on weekends with his mates, instead, he would conspicuously hang around the house when the family turned up on Saturday morning. One weekend, Mary built up the courage to talk to him, and to her surprise, he responded with great courage and showed no sign of jitteriness.

The young couple spent every weekend together pursuing recreational activities, the most pleasing of which they both enjoyed was fishing, but they had to be chaperoned by her parents when they wanted to go somewhere outside the station.

When it was revealed that Macca had been painting in his spare time, she looked forward to seeing his work, as she took a keen interest in art since the age of five. Their loving relationship was seen by all to start blossoming.

Blue and the men from the Zuckschwerdt family had been frequenting their favourite fishing spot with Blue's dad, Harry, and it could be said that, if the old blokes were to meet their maker at any time soon, that was okay by them.

News articles coming from Russia worried everyone sick. It was reported that Tsarist loyalists and military hierarchy who were guilty of terrible crimes were hunted down. Bolshevik snipers pinned them down in their hotel rooms, and knowing that their time was up, they went to the windows to receive what they hoped would be a good quick kill.

The pain of losing loved ones never went away, but the families, whose absolute faith brought them thus far, were rewarded for their faith.

Vera gave birth to Adelaide in Brisbane in 1930, and at the age of eighteen, Adelaide married my father, Walter Henry de Graaff. My name is Jon, the second of five children born to them.

Why did I write this book?

The knowledge I acquired from many camping and off-road trips was gained through life-and-death situations I encountered. If, by getting this information out to the world could save just one life, then, I will have had good reason to write it.

The many miracles that kept my family and I safe and alive on these learning adventures were so profound in that they were logic-defying. And I thought what better way to tell of them than through an Australian character who accompanied the Zuckschwerdts, my grandparents, throughout the plight of their dangerous egression from Russia.

Themes?

The pivotal themes I wanted to capture were miracles, humour, inspiration, spiritual awareness, hope, danger awareness in nature, remembering one's heritage, and faith and family.

I have seen the dangers in nature that continue to kill people while camping and four-wheel driving in Australia. My life, and that of my family, had been spared so many times that I believe that God has shown these dangers to me to warn others through this book.

When you go into the Great Outdoors, respect mother nature by seeing how she works before starting your trip. That way you will save everyone a lot of trouble, if not grief. These days I carry a PLB, Personal Locator Beacon everywhere I go, land and sea. Get them from the major camping stores. Make sure you attach them to your person when things could go wrong. Rescue is virtually guaranteed.

If you think this book has the potential to help someone, please recommend it to them. They could be interested in camping or just lovers of the Great

Outdoors, but whoever they are, they will love it. If they think otherwise, they can at least give it to someone who needs a good laugh.